Amina's Song

ALSO BY HENA KHAN

Amina's Voice

More to the Story

Zayd Saleem, Chasing the Dream

Under My Hijab

Golden Domes and Silver Lanterns: A Muslim Book of Colors

Night of the Moon: A Muslim Holiday Story

Amina's Song

Henna Khan

New York • London • Toronto • Sydney • New Delhi

An imprint of Simon & Schuster Children's Publishing Division
1230 Avenue of the Americas, New York, New York 10020

Also available in a Salaam Reads hardcover edition
Interior design by Hilary Zarycky
The text for this book was set in Adobe Garamond Pro.
Manufactured in the United States of America
0322 OFF
First Salaam Reads paperback edition April 2022
2 4 6 8 10 9 7 5 3 1
The Library of Congress has cataloged the hardcover edition as follows:
Names: Khan, Hena, author.
Title: Amina's song / Hena Khan.
Description: First edition. | New York : Salaam Reads, [2021] | Sequel to: Amina's voice. | Audience: Ages 8 to 12. | Audience: Grades 4–6. |
Summary: Feeling pulled between two cultures after a month with family in Pakistan, Amina shares her experiences with Wisconsin classmates through a class assignment and a songwriting project with new student Nico.
Identifiers: LCCN 2020009974 (print) | LCCN 2020009975 (ebook) | ISBN 9781534459885 (hardcover) | ISBN 9781534459892 (pbk) ISBN 9781534459908 (ebook)
Subjects: LCSH: Muslims—Juvenile fiction. | Pakistani Americans—Juvenile fiction. | CYAC: Muslims—Fiction. | Pakistani Americans—Fiction. | Friendship—Fiction. | Schools—Fiction. | Composition (Music)—Fiction.
Classification: LCC PZ7.K526495 Aq 2021 (print) | LCC PZ7.K526495 (ebook) | DDC [Fic]—dc23
LC record available at https://lccn.loc.gov/2020009974
LC ebook record available at https://lccn.loc.gov/2020009975

To my extended family around the globe,
whose love knows no boundaries

1

As I reach for a pair of silver earrings that my best friend, Soojin, might like, Zohra smacks my hand away.

"Don't touch anything!" she hisses.

"How am I supposed to look, then?" I laugh as I rub my wrist.

"With your eyes, and then keep walking. Tell me what you like, and I'll go back and get a good price."

"What if I want to see something up close?" The market is overflowing with a dizzying array of goods—rows of glittery bangles in every color imaginable, bolts of silky fabric, and mounds of beaded slippers, hair accessories, and evening bags. It's all screaming to be picked up, or at least photographed. I've already taken at least fifty photos and videos, and we've only been here for half an hour.

"Don't act interested in anything, Amina! And put your phone away." Zohra's tone is firm, and she suddenly sounds more like my mother than my sixteen-year-old cousin.

I glance at my older brother, Mustafa, who's walking a few paces behind us, like a bodyguard. He's dressed in dark jeans and a T-shirt, and his short scruffy beard makes him look older than Zohra, even though they're the same age.

"Do what she says." He shrugs. "You don't want to get ripped off."

I slip my phone back into my bag, resist inspecting the earrings, and keep moving. It took a bit of convincing to get Zohra to bring us here, instead of the fancy shopping center we've already been to twice in three weeks. Being there made me feel like I was back at Southridge Mall in Greendale, Wisconsin, instead of where I am: Lahore, Pakistan.

I've been wanting to visit Anarkali Bazaar despite Zohra's warnings about pushy salespeople and pickpockets. Mustafa and I grew up hearing Mama's stories about how she'd wait for school to end and catch a rickshaw here when she was a teen. When she described sharing freshly squeezed sugar-cane juice and spicy samosa plates with her girlfriends in vivid detail, I could almost taste them.

My hopes of finally tasting those things in real life were crushed when Mama cautioned, "Don't eat anything off the street" as the three of us left my uncle's home with his driver, who dropped us off at the market. Mama's worried that our American stomachs won't be able to handle anything but filtered water, home-cooked meals, and a handful of approved restaurants. That means no samosa plates from the carts we pass, no matter how incredible they smell.

"Imported from China." Zohra clicks her tongue against her teeth as she watches me eye a sparkly clip that I can picture in my friend Emily's long blond hair. "You want things made in Pakistan, don't you?"

"Yeah. Stuff my friends can't get in Greendale."

"Your friends can get anything from anywhere," Mustafa reminds me. "Thanks to something called the Internet."

"Okay, stuff they don't have, then." Mama already

bought gifts for our closest family friends, Salma Auntie and Hamid Uncle. I picked out an outfit for their daughter, Rabiya, since we have the same taste in desi clothes: nothing itchy or "auntie-looking."

Zohra links her arm with mine and navigates me through the crowds, warning me for the seventeenth time to watch my purse. I wouldn't be carrying a purse if I were wearing jeans, but I'm in a thin cotton shalwar kameez that's more comfortable in the fierce summer heat. My hand is gripping the bag that's stuffed with the money I collected from generous relatives excited to see me for the first time in eight years, and I try not to bump into people.

"Your friends will like those." Zohra points with her eyebrows toward a stall filled with colorful lacquered boxes and figurines. "They're made in Kashmir."

"They're pretty," I agree.

"Go see, but don't say anything. Once the shopkeeper hears your English, the price will triple."

I wander over and pretend to admire a shawl when I notice a green-and-gold box with a curved lid. It's shaped like a little treasure chest and would be perfect for Soojin. Then I spot some stunning jewelry in a glass case, including a silver necklace with a row of small cobalt-blue stones. I try not to stare at it.

Zohra turns to the shopkeeper after I secretly signal what I want to her.

"Bhai Sahib," she beckons in Urdu, calling the man with a mustache and thick glasses Mister Brother to be polite. "Tell me the right price for this. No ripping me off." Her tone is surprisingly aggressive.

Then Zohra picks up a candleholder, instead of the green box. When I start to protest, she gives me a death stare. I watch in silence as they haggle in Urdu over the price of something I don't want. Mister Brother claims excellent quality. My cousin complains it's robbery and says she isn't a fool. Then Zohra suddenly drops the candleholder as if she's deeply offended by it and starts to walk away.

Mustafa watches, his dark eyes amused, as Zohra yanks my arm and starts to drag me off with her.

"Sister, see this," Mister Brother offers when our backs

are turned and we're almost in the next stall. "I give you this for a good price."

Zohra turns around reluctantly.

"Don't waste our time. We're in a hurry."

"Come, see, very good price."

Zohra squeezes my arm and returns to the stall, acting like she's doing Mister Brother a favor. He shows her some bowls and gives her a number in rupees. I have no idea how much money that is since my Urdu is especially terrible when it comes to numbers. Plus, I forget how to convert Pakistani currency into dollars. Zohra shakes her head and then points toward the box I want.

"How about that? Can you live with it?" she asks me, wrinkling her nose as if it's barely worth considering.

I start to sweat.

Am I supposed to say yes or no?

I take a gamble and nod yes.

"Okay, final price. No games." Zohra challenges the shopkeeper.

The arguing continues until Mister Brother finally

gives Zohra a number she grudgingly accepts.

"What color?" she asks me. I point to the green box for Soojin and a turquoise one for Emily. Zohra adds another bright red one to the pile.

"From me to you," she says.

"What about that necklace?" I whisper to Zohra. She starts to shake her head, but Mister Brother has superhuman hearing and whips the case open and hands me the necklace before she finishes.

"Very nice," he says in English.

Zohra gives me another glare, and Mustafa starts to chuckle. I giggle too. There's no way Mister Brother hasn't figured out we aren't from here, no matter how hard Zohra tries to hide it. We've got American written all over us. Mustafa's T-shirt literally has the Captain America logo on it.

"It's very pretty," I say in my best Urdu, although I know my accent sounds pathetic. "What are these stones?"

"Lapis," Mister Brother replies in English, beaming. "Very real, very cheap."

Zohra tries to convince me to walk away again, but I won't budge.

"Can you give me your best price, please?" I imitate the Urdu phrase I've heard Zohra use. Mister Brother gives me a nod of acknowledgment, but then Zohra takes over, speaking for me. My face burns.

How am I supposed to get better at Urdu if no one lets me practice?

I can't understand everything they're saying, but it's obvious Mister Brother has the upper hand. After he names his final price, I pull out the wad of rupees from my purse, and Zohra counts some and hands them over in defeat. She won't look at me. But I take the necklace and thank the man in Urdu. And he grins like he just won the lottery.

2

"You paid way too much for that," Zohra mutters as we walk away.

"But I love it!" I rub the smooth stones of the necklace with my thumb. "I'll think of you every time I wear it."

"You might as well have picked it up and kissed it, you were so obvious," Zohra snorts.

"Seriously," Mustafa adds. "I'm surprised you didn't offer the guy more money than he asked for."

"Very funny!" I say, but I can't help smiling. I'm never going to get the hang of bargaining. I don't know how to pretend I don't like things or play the weird game of insulting something that I want. Plus, it seems wrong to argue with a grown-up.

Zohra helps me clasp the necklace around my neck and gives me a quick hug. In an instant, my fierce bargaining cousin is back to the sweet girl I've spent every minute of the last few weeks with—and begun to love like an older sister. It's hard to believe we barely knew each other when I first arrived, after only exchanging occasional gifts and letters over the years.

"Can we go now?" Mustafa asks. He's been more patient than he is when we go shopping back home. "We're supposed to meet Thaya Jaan soon."

"Don't you want to get anything?" Zohra twists her thick brown hair into a knot. When her hair is down, our family says we resemble each other, but I can't see it, even though we share the same dark eyebrows and full lips.

Mustafa shakes his head. "Nah, I took a lot of cool pics."

I realize I forgot to take more after I put my phone away and make a mental note to look at Mustafa's later. I've been sending photos and video clips to Soojin, Emily, and Rabiya so they can feel like they're here with me.

We start to head out of the market, and I hear a familiar song being played by one of the shopkeepers.

"Wait." I stop Zohra. "I've heard him before. Who is that?"

"Nusrat Fateh Ali Khan."

"Right. What kind of music is he famous for?" Baba played this singer's songs in his car when I was little, and I loved hearing the drums and clapping. At night his powerful and commanding voice would lull me to sleep.

"Qawali. It's traditional." Zohra starts to walk again, but Nusrat Fateh Ali Khan's voice stirs something inside me, and I remain standing to keep listening.

"What's he saying?" I ask.

"I don't know."

"Can you please tell me?"

Zohra stops walking and concentrates.

"Tere bin. He's saying something like 'my heart doesn't connect without you.' Or like 'my heart isn't at peace without you.'"

"Tere bin," I repeat.

"'Without you,'" she says. "Dil is 'heart.'"

I've heard a similar phrase, "dil nahi lagda," before. Mama says it sometimes. I repeat the refrain of the song in my head, so I won't forget it.

"Come on." Mustafa points to a fruit stall ahead of us. "Let's get some pomegranate juice from that guy."

"No, no, no." Zohra shakes her head. "Your mother said no bazaari food for you."

"But this is a drink. And it's fresh." Mustafa brushes off her protests and asks a man for "theen anar juice." Everyone mixes English and Urdu here, and the man nods his understanding.

The man cracks open a few pomegranates that are bursting with deep red seeds and feeds them one by one into a gigantic metal juicer that he turns with a crank. I try not to notice when he rinses the jug with tap water. Or when he pours the juice into three glasses that are murkier than they should be.

Mustafa pays for the juices with the money in his pocket

and doesn't need to ask Zohra for help translating. As we sip the sweet, tart juice through the thinnest straws ever, our cousin says a prayer aloud.

"Ya Allah, please don't let them get diarrhea."

Mustafa and I groan in disgust, and all of us crack up. My insides gurgle a little as we head to where the rickshaws are waiting, but I think it's nerves. We climb into the worn backseat of one of the three-wheeled taxis, and Zohra tells the driver where to take us. And then I brace myself for a wild ride.

I haven't gotten used to everyone driving on the opposite side of the road here yet, or all the activity on the streets. Apart from rickshaws and tons of cars, I've seen motorcycles with five people sitting on them, rumbling trucks painted in bright flower designs, and a bus packed with so many passengers that men were actually hanging off the outside. That was a video clip I sent to my friends, and they sent back emojis of shocked faces.

Today, I see the usual bicycles with riders covering their faces with scarves like bandits to keep out dust, a cart piled high with baskets of nuts pulled by a donkey, and a skinny goat that looks lost.

"Whoa," I yell as we speed through a roundabout, and I grab the handle as the driver swerves to miss a cyclist. He doesn't bother to honk, maybe because everyone else on the roads already is. We're also driving on the line separating lanes on the road instead of between them. When he was here, Baba joked that in Lahore traffic rules are more like "suggestions."

The way I feel on the roads is how I've felt in general since we arrived in this country. In some ways it's familiar and works like back home. But in other ways it's totally wild and different. The result is a mix of fun and frustrating. And no matter how much I want to fit in, sometimes I feel like I'm the only one who's holding on tight for the ride, trying not to fall out, get ripped off, or end up with diarrhea.

3

Thaya Jaan gets out of the passenger seat of his parked car as he sees us approaching. Our rickshaw drops us outside the entrance of the Wazir Khan Mosque, in front of a large brown stone gate with arches in it. My uncle's driver, Nuredin, opens the rear door of the car, and Mama comes out wearing large-framed sunglasses and a thin scarf tied at her chin.

"How was the shopping trip?" Mama asks. As she hugs me, I wonder if I also have purple juice stains like the ones I spot around Mustafa's mouth and hope she doesn't notice.

"So cool. Anarkali is awesome."

"I knew you'd like it. That's beautiful," she says, pointing to my new necklace.

Mama's dressed up for the lunch party at a cousin's house she'll go to after we visit the mosque. We agreed earlier that the rest of us could head home with Thaya Jaan instead. There won't be other kids at the lunch, and Mustafa and I need a break from nonstop parties. For the past three weeks, since we arrived in Lahore, we've been rotating through our relatives' homes for lunch, chai—which basically turns into a second lunch—and dinner.

"You're not too tired for the tour, are you, geeta?" Thaya Jaan asks me. Hearing the nickname my father gave me years ago sparks a pang of missing him. Although he arrived with us in Pakistan, Baba left last Saturday to return to work back home. The rest of us have another week in Lahore, which seems long and not long enough at the same time.

"I'm okay." I smile at my uncle, glad to see him out of the house in a freshly pressed shalwar kameez and vest with a topi pressing down his gray hair. He's as sharply dressed as he was when he visited Wisconsin last year, although he's thinner now.

Our house felt empty when Thaya Jaan left Greendale after staying with us for three months. I'd walk by the guest room expecting to see him before I remembered he was back on the other side of the world. And I couldn't believe how hard it was to see him leave, compared to how strange it had been when he first arrived. I'd felt uncomfortable around him, especially while my dad was overly focused on impressing his older brother. But that slowly changed as my uncle and I got to know each other and bonded in a way I hadn't expected.

After Thaya Jaan got sick earlier this year, my parents decided to keep our promise to visit him and finally make the trip to Pakistan this summer.

"This mosque was built during the time of the emperor Shah Jahan—who also had the Taj Mahal built. It's unique in how it blends styles from different cultures," Thaya Jaan shares as we walk through the arch. I follow Zohra's lead and cover my hair with the scarf hanging around my neck. "The restoration has been going on for more than ten years."

I hear Mustafa whistle in amazement as he sees the

mosque buildings first. I squint into the light, holding back a gasp as I take in the majestic onion-shaped domes and mustard and terra-cotta walls that connect four minarets, each topped with bright tiles. As we walk around, Thaya Jaan points to the designs on the walls and shows us different patterns like flowers and trees, almost like windows in frames. It's mesmerizing, and not like any mosque I've seen before.

I wish I had a wide-angle lens on my phone as I try to frame the mosque with light glinting off the minarets, and take a few videos instead. Zohra snaps photos of me posing in front of the most colorful areas, and then we take a few selfies, like some of the other tourists wandering around. Despite a few crowds and tour groups, there's a hush in the courtyard, and everyone whispers or speaks softly in this grand space.

"Can you imagine how gorgeous this must have been hundreds of years ago, when it was new?" Mama asks. I try, noticing how the vibrant parts of the buildings that have been restored contrast with the faint lines and weathered walls in other areas. "When I was growing up, we didn't come here, because the area was so overcrowded with shops that this part of the city was congested and hard to get through," she adds.

Thaya Jaan shows us the parts of the complex where there was a calligraphers' market in olden times, and we pause by the huge square wudu fountain in the center of the courtyard. A few men are seated with their sleeves rolled up, washing their arms and feet, and it suddenly occurs to me that the ancient mosque isn't a museum or monument. It's being used for prayers while the restoration continues.

My thoughts drift to our mosque back home and how it was shut down for more than six months after someone started a fire that destroyed parts of the interior. The building next door to it, the social hall of our Islamic Center, was trashed and marred with graffiti. Luckily, everyone in the community rushed to donate new furniture and art and worked together to cover up the horrible words that had been sprayed on the walls with fresh coats of light gray paint. But I still see them in my mind whenever I go into the hall, as much as I try not to.

"Your father said they charged the criminals who damaged your mosque," Thaya Jaan says, which means he's thinking of the same thing as me. He was visiting when the vandalism took place and was as shaken by it as the rest of us.

"Yes. That chapter can finally close," Mama says.

My stomach twists as Mama explains that the people who attacked the mosque were a bunch of teenagers, seniors in high school from Sheboygan who were eventually caught, thanks to an anonymous tip.

"They were tried," Mustafa adds, "and they might serve jail time."

"Young lives forever scarred by a foolish act." Thaya Jaan frowns.

"It was more than foolish, Thaya Jaan," Mustafa counters. "You remember how awful it was. They were charged with a hate crime."

During the trial, the vandals said they had been drinking and what started out as a stupid prank had gotten out of control. They confessed that negative things people said about Muslims in the news had riled them up and inspired the hateful words they wrote. But they claimed that the fire was an accident that wasn't supposed to happen.

I heard that one of the boys cried and said he never stopped to think about how he was hurting real people. And when the judge asked him, the boy admitted that he didn't know any Muslims personally. Their sentences could include community service, counseling, and even jail time.

"People who do terrible things aren't always evil," Thaya Jaan says. "Just misguided. May Allah have mercy on them."

I nod my head. I feel sorry for the boys, but I'm also glad they were caught. For months I imagined whoever had attacked the Islamic Center living among us and was afraid of passing them on the street or at the grocery store. The thought of seeing hate in their eyes terrified me. Mustafa told me I was being paranoid, since they had no idea who I was, and vice versa. But that didn't stop me from carrying that fear around until they were caught.

I hope they learn how wrong what they did was, and that they don't actually have to go to jail.

"Who's doing this restoration?" Mama asks. I'm glad she changed the subject and want to know the answer too.

"A team, including the Agha Khan Foundation and the American government," Thaya Jaan says. "And there's talk of making it a World Heritage site."

My heart swells to hear that people in America consider this place a historic treasure and are helping to fix it—like when so many people back home pitched in to rebuild our mosque. Soojin's church hosted our carnival and fundraiser. Emily's dad led the construction with his company. When they finished, he said the new mosque was strong enough to last for centuries. Then he joked that the supply of food in his freezer, gifts from grateful community members who cooked for his family, might last as long.

Thinking of food makes me realize I'm ready for lunch, but we enter the mosque to pray. I admire the intricate tiled ceilings and imagine artisans working together to create them. As we pray, standing in lines on red carpets, I wonder how many people have stood on this very spot, over hundreds of years. It gives me chills. I finish with the wish that nothing bad ever happen to this beautiful space.

Thaya Jann insists that Mama take the car to her cousin's house, so when we're done with the tour, the rest of us wait for an Uber.

"You kids in the mood to eat lunch out? Maybe burgers or pizza?" Thaya Jaan asks. It's like he read my mind again.

"Yes!" Mustafa and I say in unison.

"Abu!" Zohra scolds. "What about your diet?"

"One treat won't hurt me," Thaya Jaan insists as he winks at me.

Mustafa gives Thaya Jaan a high five, and we decide on KFC, which is the most popular American restaurant in Lahore. Zohra is outnumbered but doesn't seem too disappointed.

No matter how delicious it is, I'm tired of eating Pakistani food twice a day and have been craving a peanut butter and jelly sandwich for lunch instead of heavy, spicy meals. I can't think of anything better than a good old American fried chicken sandwich with some fries right now.

I love it here, but I could use a little taste of home.

4

"Why didn't you throw that before if you had it?" Zohra slaps her card on the table extra hard.

"I was saving it," I explain.

"But we could have won," Zohra moans.

I study the cards I have left in my hand, confused. I thought I had finally figured this game out.

"Let's keep going," Mustafa says.

"No use. I have these." Zohra's older brother, Ahmed, throws down the rest of the winning cards. "You girls are finished."

"Let's switch partners," Zohra suggests. "Siblings against siblings."

"No fair!" I protest. "You and Ahmed will crush us."

"It's okay, Amina," Mustafa says. "We got this."

Thaya Jaan's house has the perfect space for playing rung, or "color," the card game our cousins taught us. There's a small area upstairs with four chairs slung low to the floor and a square coffee table. Mustafa and Ahmed switch seats so Mustafa is seated across from me now.

After lunch, Thaya Jaan went to take a nap in his air-conditioned bedroom. It's blazing hot outside at midday, especially up on the roof where Zohra and I like to hang out late at night. There are a couple of charpoys up there—beds woven out of thick scratchy rope that are like shallow hammocks. We lie on them, stare at the stars, and talk about everything. In those moments, I'm more connected to her than I ever thought was possible.

That changes when she plays cards, though. Suddenly she's as cutthroat as when she bargains, and I'm a little scared of her.

Zohra deals to me, and I almost jump out of my seat with glee. I've got the ace, king, jack, and ten of diamonds!

That almost never happens. But I try to play it cool.

"Rung?" she asks me. I'm supposed to say what suit I'm picking to be the trump card before the rest of the cards are dealt.

"Hmmm." I act casual. "I guess diamonds."

"Eent," Mustafa translates for her.

"I know what diamonds are." Zohra scrunches up her face at him. She deals the rest of the cards, and I get three more diamonds. This is one of the best hands I could possibly have. I take a deep breath and make a bold move, playing the ace of diamonds first.

Mustafa inhales sharply. Zohra cackles, confident I've made a mistake. But her smirk slowly changes into a frown as round after round I drop more diamonds and force everyone to play their most valuable cards up front.

"I hope you know what you're doing," Mustafa cautions, wiping sweat off his brow.

"We got this," I promise, and when Mustafa throws down the card I was hoping for, I know we won by getting all the sets and crushing our opponents in the most humiliating way.

"Wow." Zohra seems genuinely impressed as Mustafa and I celebrate. "You destroyed us. Don't worry—we'll get you back."

But before we can start another round, Mama calls from downstairs. She's returned from her lunch party, and it's time for chai. Thaya Jaan is freshly washed up, and my aunt, who we call Thayee, rolls out the tea trolley.

The teapot is sitting under a thick quilted dome to keep it piping hot. It's surrounded by bowls of coarse white sugar and lumps of natural brown sugar, and various cookies, fruits, and sweets arranged on plates.

Thayee says the British invented high tea, but Indians and Pakistanis perfected it. That's because our tea is rich and milky with spices in it, and our sweets are nutty, moist, and decadent.

"I still have those sandwiches sitting in me." Mustafa shakes his head when Thayee offers him some sliced mango.

"What sandwiches?" Mama asks. "Where did you eat?"

"KFC."

Mama and Thayee grumble their disapproval, but

Mustafa and I grin at each other. Since neither of us drinks tea, Thayee makes us hot chocolate, which I drink to be polite. The milk here tastes different and feels thicker somehow. It's got a distinct scent, especially when warmed, that the chocolate doesn't fully mask. I do love the rectangular chocolate sandwich cookies, though, and pile a few on my plate, making a mental note to take a few packages with us when we go home. We won't be allowed to bring back the food I've enjoyed the most, summer-ripe mangos that ooze sweetness. So instead I'm devouring as many as I can and trying to imprint the taste in my memory.

"How did it go today?" Thaya Jaan asks Ahmed. My cousin, who's in medical school, is doing a rotation at a clinic in the mornings, hanging out with us in the afternoons, and studying at night. He and Mustafa play a lot of cricket, too.

While my cousin talks to Thaya Jaan about his patients, I tune out, eat my mangos, and watch Mustafa, who's leaning back on the sofa and reading on his phone. I haven't gotten used to seeing him with a proper beard, although there are patches on the sides of his mouth where it hasn't grown in fully. His hair is longer than it used to be too, and he either lets it go wild or slicks it back. Since he's been working out lately, he's almost too big for the furniture. But in addition to his size, Mustafa's personality fills whatever room he's in. Everyone here loves him, and he seems more comfortable in his skin than I am in mine.

I pull out my phone too and start to record the scene.

"Chai time," I narrate as I pan across the room.

"You're recording this, too?" Mustafa asks. "When are you going to watch all of these videos again?"

I don't answer but zoom in on his face, which he covers with his hand. I've got lots of clips like these that I've recorded over the past few weeks, but it doesn't feel like enough. I want to take all of our trip back home with me—every moment, conversation, taste, and scent—even though I know I can't.

Zohra is chatting with Mama and Thayee about something funny on YouTube featuring the different types of annoying drivers on the road. She gets up and imitates the host and makes a joke in Urdu. While the rest of the family laughs, I smile awkwardly, because I don't get the punch line.

That's how it often is when we all sit around together. It becomes obvious that I don't quite fit in with my relatives, although the same blood runs through my veins. I don't share their language, their sense of humor, or their memories. When someone busts out with an expression, or a line of poetry, and everyone chimes in with a laugh or comment, I can't help but feel like an impostor, or a shapeshifter who appears to be a regular Pakistani girl on the outside but doesn't know how to act like one.

As if she can read my mind, Zohra translates the joke for me, which is something about catching a chicken. I appreciate her trying but wish I could understand Urdu enough to get it on my own. Plus, it doesn't make a whole lot of sense in English.

"Why the long face, Amina?" Thaya Jaan asks me from

across the room. I shake my head, unable to explain and not sure how to respond.

"Are you thinking of how much you'll miss us when you go home?" Zohra guesses.

I nod yes, and though I wasn't thinking that before, suddenly I am. I want more time here, to learn Urdu and to be surrounded by people who love me so much, impostor or not.

"What are you going to miss the most?" Thayee asks me. She's the person I've spent the least amount of time with on this trip, quiet and thoughtful, and a retired college professor always busy with charity work. I don't know how to explain that I'm going to miss the memories I haven't had a chance to make yet, with people who I want to be a constant part of my life and see more than once every eight years. My throat tightens, and I'm afraid I'll start crying, so I quickly list the first things that I can think of.

"I'll miss hearing the adhan and the neighbor's roosters. And eating these mangos. And even that annoying commercial for tissue paper that comes on TV all the time."

"What about me?" Zohra asks with a teasing grin.

"I'll miss beating you in rung," I reply. And then I quickly take a sip of my hot chocolate and hide my face in the cup, before tears start falling. Because I'm going to miss her more than I want to think about right now.

5

"Ooooh. That smells so good." I inhale deeply.

"Raat ki raani," Zohra says from the charpoy she's sprawled across on the rooftop terrace. "It's called queen of the night, since it blooms after dark."

Even two stories above the garden, the fragrance fills the air around us. It's late, after ten o'clock, and everything is quieting down for the night. I hear less honking in the distance, and fewer lights interfere with the stars. One of the stray cats that Zohra feeds is curled up on the roof near the leg of my charpoy, asleep, but I'm not sleepy at all. Zohra and I are settling in for our nightly chat.

"I love the scent. I want to plant some in Greendale.

But I wonder if it would survive in the winter," I say.

"Doubt it. It likes hot weather. I wonder if *I* would survive your winter, but I want to see the snow," Zohra replies. She drops the shells of the pistachios she's eating into a metal bowl.

"You should come visit us in the winter." I sit up at the idea of Zohra in my hometown and the chance to show her what our lives are like in America. I could introduce her to Rabiya, Soojin, and Emily, who I know will adore her. And Zohra would love checking out the museums and the mall and all the Christmas decorations and lights.

"Maybe. I don't know." Zohra sounds surprisingly uninterested.

"You and Ahmed should come together," I press. "Isn't he almost twenty? You're old enough to travel alone."

"He has his second year of medical school starting in September, and I have school too. I don't think we can."

"You have winter break, don't you?"

"Yes." Zohra pauses. "But we won't get American visas. It took Abu years to get his. And your government is even more strict about letting young people into the country."

"Why?"

Zohra hands me the bowl of nuts, but I wave it away.

"Because they think we won't leave. That we say we're coming for a visit, but it's a trick so we can stay forever." Zohra grumbles and shakes her head. "But not everyone wants to live in America. I know I don't."

Zohra's last few words cut through the warm night air.

What's wrong with living in America?

"I like my life here," Zohra continues. "I want to be close to the family. I want to work for my country and do something to help people here. And I don't want to be in a place where I'm not wanted."

Heat rises to my face as she utters the last sentence. She's talking about *my* country, the one that's a part of me and made me who I am. I stay silent and stare at the sky, trying to make out constellations as I think about how to respond.

"You're not 'not wanted' in America," I finally say in a small voice that sounds less confident than I want.

"I listen to the news, Amina," Zohra scoffs. "Remember

what happened to your own mosque. And the things those kids wrote on the walls."

"But stuff like that isn't happening all the time!" I argue, even as the words "GO HOME" flash through my mind.

Zohra doesn't respond, but I can sense her disbelief.

"Most Americans are nice, and good," I continue. "Everyone helped repair the mosque. My friend Soojin's church held our carnival and everything."

"They wouldn't have needed to if it wasn't destroyed in the first place."

I gulp. That's true too. But I know Zohra is wrong. I just don't know how to make her see it. My cousin is fierce and loving, and loyal and generous. But when she speaks like I'm a silly little kid and she's an authority, it's like we're back at the market. I'm supposed to stay quiet and not have opinions.

"You know, I was afraid to come here," I say after a moment.

"What?"

"To Pakistan. I was afraid to come."

"You're only saying that now, because of what I said." As she dismisses my thoughts, Zohra turns her body so her back is toward me. It's a slight movement, but suddenly the distance between us is as wide as the ocean that usually separates us.

"No. It's true. I heard scary things about terrorism, and explosions and stuff, and I was afraid something bad would happen to us while we were here."

Zohra snorts. The cat stirs, stretches, and then curls herself back into a ball.

"I'm just saying that you can't always think everything is what you hear on the news," I continue, realizing Baba said something similar to me a few months ago. When my father sensed that I wasn't excited about visiting Pakistan, he urged me to talk about why. I finally confessed my fears to him one night, and he gave me a lecture about "being rational" and not letting my fears limit me.

"What are you supposed to believe, then?" Zohra asks.

Baba told me there's a lot beyond headlines we read, and so much I don't know about this country. He pointed out that people mostly hear and remember bad news. It's true. I've never heard a news story about people in Pakistan sitting around drinking chai and making jokes. And I was surprised to see how happy the people who live in Pakistan are and how their lives are as full as mine. In some ways, with all of the family around and the constant commotion, they might seem a little fuller.

"There's good and bad everywhere," I finally say. "That's what Baba says."

"My abu says that too," Zohra agrees. "I guess they *are* brothers."

Our fathers live on different continents and only see each other after years, but in some ways they are strikingly similar. And in other ways, total opposites. Like Zohra and me, too.

"Can you sing something for me?" Zohra surprises me with the question after a moment of us being quiet in our own thoughts.

"What?"

"I heard you singing in the shower. What was it?"

"Nothing." As my cheeks heat up again, I'm relieved it's dark enough so Zohra can't see. Earlier I was belting out lyrics to the Stevie Wonder song I'd been learning to play on the piano before we left home. I was certain the thick walls of Thaya Jaan's house and running water were loud enough to drown me out.

"I've never heard you sing properly." Zohra sits up.

"Maybe later," I say, stalling. "I can't remember all the words."

"Come on, sing me something," Zohra presses. "How about Taylor Swift?"

"How about someone else?"

"But she's so talented. Why do you listen to such budee music, Amina?" This isn't the first time Zohra has complained about my "old lady" music.

"I listen to everything," I insist. I can't explain my love for classic soul and Motown to my cousin. She doesn't like the older artists who sing about things with so much passion and depth in their voices that it makes me feel more alive. Like Stevie Wonder. Aretha Franklin. And Al Green.

Zohra pulls up Taylor Swift on YouTube and starts to sing along with her off-key. I chime in, to prove I can enjoy it too.

"Me-ee-ee-ee," we sing together, and start to laugh. The gulf between us is gone. We scroll through a bunch of other videos and sing to them until we're tired and thirsty. It reminds me of hanging out with Rabiya back home, and her pushing me to record myself singing and post it online.

"I want you to visit us and meet my friends," I say as Zohra starts to gather her things. "And to have a big snowball fight and go cross-country skiing and drink real hot chocolate."

"What's real hot chocolate?" Zohra reminds me that I've been drinking Thayee's version for weeks.

"I mean hot chocolate with marshmallows. You don't put marshmallows in yours," I quickly add as I pet the cat, who is now rubbing against the leg of the charpoy.

"Marshmallows?" Zohra asks.

"They're fluffy clouds of sugar, like little pillows."

"I know what marshmallows are," Zohra says, laughing. "I just didn't know you put them in chocolate."

"It's the best." I explain how they melt into a layer of gooey goodness, and Zohra seems a little more interested.

"Maybe one day I'll come to America," she says as we walk back into the house arm in arm. "But just for a visit."

I hope she will. And if she does, I know she'll end up loving it, as much as I love being here.

6

"It's never going to fit." Mama shakes her head at the heap of things on the floor that we have to squeeze into our suitcases.

"Take one of ours," Thayee suggests. "We have extras."

"Thank you. But then we'll have to pay for excess baggage." Mama frowns.

"Why don't you trade that smaller suitcase for a bigger one I have?" Thayee offers.

The smaller suitcase is mine, and I've already shoved everything I could inside it, including gifts and snacks that Zohra and Ahmed kept adding.

One thing I didn't have to pack is the set of silver bangles that Zohra gave me last night. For weeks I'd admired the ones that jingle lightly on her wrist. She surprised me by taking off half and slipping them onto mine.

"Okay, let's swap out the bags," Mama sighs. "Amina, can you get Mustafa to put yours up on the bed? My back is sore."

"I can do it," I volunteer.

I hoist the suitcase onto the bed, unzip it, and, as I start to empty it, see another gift inside, carefully wrapped up in a shawl. It's a Quran that Thaya Jaan gave me—the one he read from when he was a boy. Its burgundy cover is worn around the edges, and the pages are super thin, almost like rice paper.

I refused to take it at first, saying it belonged with him or his children instead of me. But Thaya Jaan insisted that he wanted me to have it. He said he was proud of how far I'd come in my study of the Quran since he visited. I practiced reading with him most mornings on this trip, like I did when I was preparing for the recitation competition last year, and never got tired.

Ever since Thaya Jaan first led prayers in our house in Greendale, and I discovered how beautiful his voice is, I've wanted to be able to recite Quran as well as him. I listen to famous qaris with my headphones and try to mimic their inflections and elongations of words when I'm alone. It's helping me memorize new surahs and cement in my mind the ones I used to forget. Sister Naima at Sunday school compliments me more than ever, but I'm not doing it for her. I'm doing it for me. Plus, the next time there's a Quran competition, I'll be ready.

Tucked next to the Quran is a stack of postcards of the Wazir Khan Mosque. Mama bought them for me to put in little frames and hang in my room. My favorite is the close-up shot of tiled calligraphy in blue and white.

Thinking of my bedroom makes it real—we're leaving tonight, at three a.m. Like a punch in the gut, it hits me that in a few hours I will say good-bye to my family to get on a long, cramped plane ride across the world. Now that the day has arrived, I'm not ready to go. I begged Mama to extend our trip yesterday. But Baba is waiting for us at home, and I start school in a week. Like Mama said, we have no choice but to leave.

I texted Soojin and Emily this morning, which made me feel a little better.

Me: I'm leaving today. Sad to go.

Soojin: I can't wait to see you!!!! It feels like forevvvvvvver!

Emily: Me too! See you soon!!!! ♥

We all gather later than usual to eat the special dinner Thayee planned for us. It's a mix of so many dishes, I don't know where to start. But tonight I'm hungry for them all, since I don't know when I'll taste these foods again. Mustafa's plate is piled extra high too.

Thaya Jaan doesn't eat much but smiles at me tenderly and fills up my water glass.

"You will write to me, geeta?" he asks.

"Of course," I say. "Or we can just FaceTime."

That makes him chuckle.

"That too."

"When will you visit us again, Thaya Jaan?" I've been thinking about it every day but haven't been able to bring myself to ask him.

Thaya Jaan shakes his head slightly.

"Allah knows best. I'd love to come, but I need to get stronger. Pray for me."

I nod. That wasn't the answer I was hoping for.

"But I want to see you again." I squash a chickpea on my plate with a piece of roti.

"You will, insha'Allah," Thaya Jaan says. "I'm so happy that you enjoyed your trip here, and that you've made such a strong connection with everyone."

I nod again. My throat feels like I swallowed a balloon, and I can't speak.

"This is your home too, and you are always welcome here. And in the meantime, I want you to do something for me," Thaya Jaan says.

I expect him to say something about reading a little bit from his Quran each day. He already said that earlier, and I promised to try. He probably forgot we already discussed it, like he does sometimes.

"I want you to show people in America the beauty of Pakistan. They don't know this place like you do now."

What? How in the world am I supposed to do that?

Mustafa is sitting on the other side of Thaya Jaan, and he speaks up.

"We're going to teach our friends back home how to play rung," he volunteers. We decided that Rabiya and her older brother, Yusuf, would make great opponents.

"You can use the practice," Ahmed teases.

"What about cricket?" Thayee asks.

Mustafa has a cricket bat in his luggage, which meant giving away half the clothes he brought with him to make room for it. He and Ahmed were playing in the yard this evening after the sun went down, and they tried unsuccessfully to get Zohra and me to join them.

"All of those are good things." Thaya Jaan sits back, and I think he's satisfied with our plan. But then he asks me again directly, "You will, Amina?"

"I will," I promise him, hoping I can keep my word. I gulp down some water and finish what's on my plate.

When we're done with dessert, it's almost eleven p.m., and all we have left to do is load up the cars and say our farewells. Ahmed is taking us to the airport with a cousin of

Mama's in a second car because of the luggage. We gather in front of the house, and as we stand around, I take deep breaths of the raat ki raani, which seems extra fragrant tonight.

"Thank you for everything," I start to say to Thayee, but she cuts me off with a cluck of her tongue.

"Nothing to thank us for," she says, enveloping me in a hug.

"I'll miss you," I say to Zohra before she grabs me and squeezes me tight. We both tear up and start to giggle at the same time.

"You better." She smiles. "Don't forget us when you get back to your friends and your life in America."

"I won't."

Thaya Jaan is last, and I almost can't bear to say goodbye to him. I walk over to him and stand there awkwardly, and he reaches out and pats my cheek. And then he opens up his arms slightly, and I dive in for a hug. Neither of us says anything, and after a while he kisses my forehead and lets go.

Ahmed opens up the car door and says we should get going, so I quickly crawl into the backseat of the car before I start to seriously cry. Mustafa gets in next to me, and Mama squeezes in on his other side. I'm surprised when Mustafa puts his arm around me, and I rest my head on his shoulder and let a few tears fall. He's sad to be leaving too. We all are.

"Let's go, please," Mama says to Nuredin, who backs the car out of the driveway and through the gate.

Thaya Jaan, Thayee, and Zohra are like statues, their arms raised in farewell, until the big green gate closes behind us.

7

I'm strapped in my seat next to Mustafa for our second flight, from Paris to Chicago. My headphones are on so I can start a movie immediately after the safety announcements. But first I have to sit through a video of smiling flight attendants doing a choreographed dance while they fasten and unfasten seat belts and sashay along the illuminated path to the exits while I hear instructions in English and French. Finally, it's over, and I can scroll through the film choices.

Mustafa selects a superhero movie on his screen.

"That one again?" I ask. "You've seen it a million times."

"Yup." Mustafa slips his headphones on and tunes me out as his movie begins. As I watch him, I wonder if the closeness we shared on the trip will last after we get home. Although I spent most of my time with Zohra, Mustafa and I bonded in a way we haven't in a while. He could simply make eye contact, and I'd know exactly what he was thinking. We shared inside jokes and whispered about things we didn't understand. It felt like he was watching out for me, and he paid more attention to me than he usually does at home.

Even though I'm sitting next to him, I kind of miss him already.

"What?" Mustafa turns to me because I'm still staring at him.

"Nothing."

I'm surprised to see one of the movie choices is an old Indian film called *Amar Akbar Anthony*. Zohra turned it on one night after we couldn't agree on anything else to watch and said it was her father's favorite. She tried to explain its totally unbelievable plot. Like how three brothers who are adopted by three different families—one Muslim, one Hindu, and one Christian—could discover each other as grown-ups and team up to save a woman who gets kidnapped. In the end, I liked it, and the songs got stuck in my head for days afterward. I turn it on to listen to the music and watch the dancing and funny parts again.

"Watch your elbows, please." A flight attendant rolls a cart down the aisle with what I guess is supposed to be lunch. Mixed with someone's perfume and the stale airplane air, the smell makes my stomach lurch.

"Chicken or pasta?" the flight attendant, her face bright with makeup and false lashes, asks me.

"No thank you."

"You sure, hon?"

"Yes." I'm not hungry after devouring two croissants and a thick hot chocolate at the airport in Paris.

"Why don't you take the tray?" she insists. Before I can refuse, she slaps a tray down on my table. It's got a roll, carrot salad, and some kind of sponge cake on it. I nibble on the bread and a soft cheese wedge and watch my movie, marveling over the fact that I actually picked an Indian movie over all the American choices.

DING! The seat belt light goes on and the movie pauses while the captain warns us about turbulence ahead. Mustafa's watching a fighting scene and is unfazed. But I clutch his arm as the plane bounces enough for me to make sure my belt is tight around my waist.

"It's okay." Mama peers over at me from the other side of Mustafa. "Just a few bumps."

I say a prayer anyway and, when the movie ends, put on music to relax. For the next couple of hours I'm lost in the sounds of a playlist I named Through the Decades. It's got my favorite songs from the sixties through the nineties, including Motown classics, soul, and R&B. I listen to it on shuffle and never get tired of it.

I think about what Zohra said about my listening to old lady music. My friend Rabiya says the same thing. It's partly my music teacher Ms. Holly's fault for getting me hooked on it last year when she was trying to get me to sing for our winter recital.

Ms. Holly also gave me blank sheet music and encouraged me to compose original songs on the piano. I played around with melodies but never thought anything was worth writing down. I also hadn't thought of adding lyrics before. But ever since the night I sang on the roof with Zohra, words to my own song—fragments and phrases—have been dancing through the back of my mind. It's a jumble inspired by artists I admire and by all the emotion swirling inside me.

Watching regular people sing famous artists' songs on YouTube is cool, especially when they cover someone else's song well. But it's entirely different to sing your own song, the one that comes from your heart. I haven't been able to get my melodies or my lyrics to work, though, and don't know if I'll ever be able to make a listener feel what I do.

"You have to put your seat up." Mustafa jostles me. "We're landing."

I yank up my seat and check my seat belt as the plane makes its descent. I'm always extra tense until I hear the whine of the plane's wheels coming down. Then I hold my breath and wait for the plane to touch down.

"You okay?" Mustafa pokes me. "You're not going to throw up, are you?"

"No."

"Want some gum?"

"Yeah."

Mustafa hands me a piece and pops some in his mouth.

"It's weird to be going home," he says.

"I know."

"I can't believe we start school in a week. The trip flew by. It didn't seem like a whole month."

"I miss everyone already," I say, fumbling with the buckle on my seat belt.

"Me too."

It's not much of a conversation, but enough to make me wonder if Mustafa is as mixed up as I am, as we travel not only through time zones but also from one part of our lives to another.

The plane lands with a few bumps, and as we race along the runway, the forces of the plane's momentum and the brakes oppose each other. My insides go in one direction while my body careens forward, and I grasp the seat as we start to slow down. We made it.

Mama looks as exhausted as I feel as we file off the plane and get into a line marked US CITIZENS. Half the plane goes into the VISITORS line. When the man in a blue uniform and a bored expression finally calls us up to the desk, I hold my breath. He studies the photo in my passport and then stares at me. I don't smile, since I'm not smiling in my passport photo either. They told me not to when we got them taken, but Mustafa says that makes it look like a mug shot.

The man turns to Mustafa next, glancing back and forth at him and then at his passport. In his photo, Mustafa is a boy, not the gigantic bearded guy standing here now. Finally, the man stamps all of our passports and winks at me as he hands them back to Mama.

"Welcome home," he says. "Good to have you back."

His simple words make the smile that's missing in my photo appear on my face. Suddenly it *is* good to be back, to be home.

8

I'm wide awake although it's the middle of the night. I try to resist looking at the clock again.

3:56 a.m.

Last time I checked, it was 3:49 a.m.

If this is jet lag, it isn't fun.

Yesterday, when we finally collected our luggage and passed through Customs, we found Baba waiting outside the international arrivals gate at Chicago O'Hare Airport. It reminded me of waiting in the same spot for Thaya Jaan when he came to visit us, almost a year ago.

I spotted Baba first when the doors opened. His face lit up and he rushed toward us, and soon I was crushed in a big group hug. It felt great, until I remembered that we had to get into the minivan and drive for another hour and a half to get home.

Baba wanted to talk, but I was too exhausted to say much. Mama filled him in on the last couple of days of our trip while Mustafa dozed, and I stared out the window. The highway seemed empty after the streets of Lahore, and it was so quiet it was almost eerie. There was no honking or the hum of motorcycles or the music that seemed to fill the streets.

Had there been actual music, or was I hearing it in my head?

Our house seemed smaller when we walked in, and it smelled different than I remembered it. I left my shoes by the front door and noticed how tidy Baba had kept everything. No one was very hungry for the dinner he heated for us, but he said we should try to eat since it was dinnertime. I forced myself to take a few bites. Then I took a quick shower and got into my pajamas. Baba told me to stay up a little later when I said good night, insisting that I shouldn't go to sleep too early or my jet lag would be worse. But all I wanted was to lie down flat and close my eyes.

Now I'm awake while I'm supposed to be asleep, staring at the plastic glow-in-the-dark stars on my ceiling and wishing I had listened to him. Is this the same time that I would be under the real stars back in Lahore, chatting with Zohra on the roof, lying on our charpoys? I start to calculate: Four a.m. here means . . . two p.m. in Pakistan. Zohra's probably getting dried fruit from the kitchen like she would when she craved something sweet after lunch. I wonder if that's what she's doing now and realize that I have no idea what my cousin's regular life is like. For the past month she was focused on entertaining me. We went from party to party to meet relatives, to restaurants and shops, and to sites like the mosques, gardens, and the Lahore Fort. We played cards and watched movies and talked all night. What's she doing now that we're gone, and her life is supposed to go back to normal too?

I grab my phone and flip through the photos and videos in the shared album from our trip that Mustafa created.

Zohra and I took a ton of silly shots, and I'm surprised he didn't delete our worst selfie fails. I scroll through the images of the Wazir Khan Mosque and study the ones Mustafa took in Anarkali. There's one of Zohra talking to Mister Brother that makes me smile. It seems so long ago, although barely a week has passed since that day. But even though there are hundreds of photos and dozens of videos, they don't begin to capture all the memories of our trip.

Next I rummage through my desk for an old spiral notebook with only a couple of used pages. I scribble the word "PRIVATE" across the front with a marker and tear out the old notes. It's as good as new. I find a scented purple pen and start to write about my trip, random thoughts and memories that I can maybe turn into lyrics later. I include phrases in Urdu like "ye ha," which means "this is," that Zohra used to say all the time, and new words I learned and don't want to forget.

My stomach rumbles and my head begins to hurt, so I put the notebook away and head downstairs to find something to eat. The lights are on in the kitchen, and Mustafa is already in there, sitting with a big bowl of cereal and reading on his phone.

"Can't sleep either?" he asks me.

"I've never been so awake in my life."

Mustafa grimaces.

"Want some cereal? Milk in America is the greatest thing ever." He pushes the gallon jug toward me.

"You sound like a Wisconsin dairy ad. They'd be so proud."

"I'm serious. And this cereal is amazing."

I get a bowl and pour myself some of the cereal with almonds and dried berries and add milk. Mustafa's right. There's something extra comforting and delicious about the cool milk and crispy flakes.

We crunch in silence for a while. Mustafa's amused by something on his phone and starts to type. It's like I'm not there anymore.

"I wonder what Zohra is doing," I say.

"Why don't you ask her?" Mustafa says, still looking at his phone. "Video chat her."

"Right now?"

"Why not?"

I try to imagine it. What if we have nothing to say to each other? What if it isn't the same with all this distance between us?

Mustafa gets up and puts his bowl in the dishwasher.

"I've already been texting with Ahmed for the past hour," he says. "They're at home chilling. I'm going to try to sleep. You good?"

"Yeah."

I get Mama's iPad from the family room, where she charges it, take a deep breath, and try to connect with Zohra. It rings and rings and says "unavailable." I try again, remembering that she isn't always close to a phone. On the third try it connects, but instead of Zohra, Thaya Jaan's bearded face fills the screen.

"Amina! Assalaamualaikum."

"Walaikum assalaam," I reply. Thaya Jaan looks older than he does in real life, like the camera added ten years. I can tell he's sitting in his favorite chair in the family room and guess that he recently finished saying his prayers and is reading Quran. I wish I were sitting next to him.

"You made it home safely, Alhamdulillah. How was the journey?"

"Long."

"What time is it there?"

"Like four thirty in the morning."

"Jet-lagged, I see. It will take some days to get back to your schedule."

Zohra squeezes into the screen next to her father and smiles.

"Amina, I miss you!"

"I miss you, too. What are you guys doing?"

"We're not guys," Zohra laughs, and I remember I told her about how my parents always say that to us since "guy" means "cow" in Urdu. She takes the phone so it's all her face filling the screen now. Her eyes are clear despite the grainy video.

"Right."

"It's too quiet here without you. The house is so empty. Abu and I are sitting here being sad."

"Really?" The thought of them missing us makes me happier.

"And I have to get ready for school, and I'm not ready at all to go study."

Zohra mentioning school reminds me that I'm starting seventh grade in a week and haven't done anything to prepare. Mama said we'll go back-to-school shopping in the next couple of days, but I can't even begin to process that. Plus, my summer math packet sits unfinished in my backpack. I have at least five pages left.

"Did anything break in your luggage?" Zohra asks. "When are you going to give your friends their gifts?"

"I didn't open my bag yet. I hope not." I let out an enormous yawn.

"You should sleep," Zohra says.

"After fajr prayer." I hear Thaya Jaan's voice.

"Okay."

"But call me tomorrow." Zohra puts her head next to her father's so I can see them both again. They wave to me while Zohra blows me kisses.

"I'll try. Khuda hafiz," I say, and then I press the end button and sit for a moment with the tablet. My family in Pakistan is still there, even if I'm here.

I think back to our last night on the roof, when Zohra grabbed my hand and asked, "You're not going to forget me when you go back to America, are you?"

I told her she was being silly and promised I wouldn't. And then I tried to say the refrain from "Tere Bin," but it came out wrong, and I ended up saying something about burning lentils. We both laughed until we cried.

I don't want them to forget me—terrible Urdu and all. I'm going to find a way to make sure that they, and Pakistan, stay a big part of my life. And I have to make sure others understand what an amazing place it is, like I promised my uncle I would.

9

“What about this one? It’s cute.” Mama holds up a long skirt with ruffles on it that would be perfect if I was living in the 1850s and had a matching bonnet to go along with it.

I shake my head.

Mama sighs and turns back to the rack, yanking each hanger across the bar with a little more force than before.

“This?” she asks. She pulls out a light blue denim shirt with snaps on the pockets.

“Maybe.” I could wear that.

This has been going on for the past half hour. Mama shows me things that are either straight from the Middle

Ages or designed for someone who's middle-aged. Whatever I like gets raised eyebrows or a frown.

I find some cute printed leggings.

"I like these," I say.

"You'll need to wear a long shirt on top. Something to cover your bottom."

All the T-shirts in my pile barely hit my waist.

"I don't understand why everything is so tiny. You know, less isn't always more," Mama grumbles.

"What?"

"You're a reflection of your parents. And I don't want you running around half naked. It's not necessary. You can be fashionable, and decent."

Mama says stuff like that, but then she's too impatient to search for cute things that she considers decent. Her best friend Salma Auntie is way more into shopping. She and Rabiya were supposed to join us at the mall, and I wish they were here to help. But Auntie texted Mama saying they were delayed at the dentist, and that they'll meet us for lunch afterward. I'm ready to eat already. Negotiating with Mama over my wardrobe has been way more stressful than haggling over prices in the market in Pakistan.

Mama finds a shirt she calls a tunic that resembles a kameez I wore in Pakistan. It's white and has light blue embroidery around the neckline.

"How about this? With jeans?" she asks.

"Yeah, I like that," I agree.

We go through all of my selections next. Anything that doesn't cover at least half my butt goes straight into the "no" pile. I didn't bother picking out any tank tops or sleeveless shirts since Mama doesn't let me wear those. But now she frowns at a couple of short-sleeved tops I picked.

"That's barely a sleeve," she grumbles. "How is that a sleeve?"

Her other issue is shirts that fit tight. Mama says they are too clingy.

I pick up a pair of jeans that are frayed on the bottom and have a few holes in them, and am about to show them to Mama, until I think better of it. I can already hear her exclaim, "Why in the world do they make clothes with holes in them?"

In Pakistan I saw enough kids in tattered clothes with their hands outstretched to finally understand why my parents always insist that Mustafa and I don't leave the house in anything torn or dirty.

The first time a little boy in a filthy blue T-shirt and flip-flops approached me outside a shopping center in Lahore, I froze. He called me "sister" in Urdu and motioned toward his mouth. I wanted to help him but didn't have any money or food on me. With a lump in my throat, I turned to Zohra, who gently told him, "Forgive us," and continued walking.

"Can't we help him?" I whispered to her as we passed.

"Not like that." Zohra shook her head sadly. "Most of the time, if you give kids on the street money, the adults who are making them beg take it. And it encourages them to put more kids on the streets, instead of in school where they belong."

She explained that it's better to give money to local

groups who make sure it actually goes toward feeding, educating, and housing poor people. And she promised it was a better option. It didn't stop my stomach from constricting like it was being squeezed through a hand crank every time I saw someone like that little boy for the rest of the trip. Thinking of him now fills me with guilt.

How is it fair that I have a life like this, and someone like him has so little?

"This is enough," I tell Mama, pointing to the pile of items we have.

"If you need more, we can come back," Mama says, looking relieved.

Mustafa returns from the young men's section with an armload of clothes for himself. Mama rifles through it and objects to a couple of T-shirts that are too expensive, or too ugly, and we head to the checkout.

The cashier gives us a coupon for 20 percent off, but when I see the total, which is still a lot of money, I gulp and thank Mama for the new clothes. Then we head to the food court next to the movie theater, where Auntie and Rabiya are waiting for us. I spot Rabiya in front of the teriyaki noodle place, nibbling a free sample off a toothpick.

"Welcome back!" Salma Auntie says, coming over with a big smile.

"How was the trip?" Rabiya gives me a hug and hands me another sample.

"Great," I reply as I chew, not knowing where to begin. I was in touch with Rabiya while we were away and sent her a few videos and photos, but now I have no idea what else to share. We get our food and settle into a table. As we eat, Mama starts telling stories, and Mustafa and I jump in and fill in the gaps.

"My cousin Zohra is the best," I say to Rabiya during a pause in the conversation. "You'd love her so much."

Rabiya nods and slurps up her noodles.

"She's like us, but different, and so smart," I continue. "These are some of her bangles—she gave them to me when we left so we can be twins."

"Cool." Rabiya glances at the bangles and then continues to eat, but something in her expression changes.

"I want her to visit us so bad. It would be awesome if she came here! I know she'd love it."

Rabiya puts down her fork, takes a sip of her drink, and doesn't say anything. I can't read her eyes, but it looks something like disappointment or annoyance.

Is she jealous of Zohra?

I was planning to show Rabiya some of my favorite pictures of Zohra and me on my phone, but I change the subject. Rabiya's always been the closest thing to a younger sister I've had in my life. Maybe she doesn't like hearing me gush about someone else?

"Mustafa and I want to show you and Yusuf how to play rung," I say instead.

"Oh, we already know how. It's so fun." Rabiya perks up, and I decide that I must be right about her feelings, even as I swallow my own regret over not being able to talk about Zohra with her.

"Well then, we challenge you," Mustafa declares.

"You won't be able to beat us," Rabiya warns.

As she trash-talks Mustafa, I notice things about Rabiya

I haven't paid attention to before. Like the way she always wears a little gold Allah charm from Pakistan around her neck and the easy way she switches between English and Urdu when talking to her mom and mine. Why didn't my parents make sure I knew how to speak Urdu as well as Rabiya?

"No one ever let me speak Urdu in Pakistan," I blurt out.

"What are you talking about?" Mama says. "Everyone told you to speak in Urdu the whole time we were there."

"Well, they said that. But then they laughed at me whenever I tried. Or they spoke for me. And they talked to me in English mostly."

"I don't think they meant it in a bad way." Mama frowns. "They probably wanted you to understand."

"They like speaking in English, too," Mustafa adds. "They watch all those English shows and YouTubers and love everything about America."

"Most things," I correct, but the shape-shifter feeling is back.

After we finish eating, we walk to the parking lot

together, and Mustafa loads our bags into the trunk. Mama pulls out the gifts we brought, and Salma Auntie starts to argue that it's too much before she knows what's inside. Rabiya squeals as she unwraps her package and holds up her outfit, which is extra sparkly in the garage light.

"I'm going to save it for Eid," she adds, which means she definitely likes it.

"Ready for a new school year, Amina?" Salma Auntie asks me after hugging and scolding Mama at the same time. "Tenth grade for you already, Mustafa?"

"Yeah," we both mumble.

"The kids are jet-lagged," Mama explains. "They were up again before six today."

That's true. But I think I'm suffering from more than jet lag. The part of my brain that regulates time definitely hasn't adjusted to being back yet, but neither has the rest of me. It's like a piece of me was left in Pakistan, and I wonder when I'll be whole again.

10

HONK!

I run outside the house as Soojin's van pulls up. The passenger door opens, and Soojin pops out, tanner and taller than when I last saw her. She's wearing an outfit I haven't seen before, a tank top that says FIERCE and jean shorts that are shredded around the pockets. She looks ready to hit the beach compared to me, in my track pants and loose T-shirt. Mrs. Park doesn't have the same rules about clothing as my mom.

"Hey!" Soojin gives me a big squeeze. "I missed you!"

"I missed you, too," I say as I crawl into the backseat. "Your hair got so long." Soojin's ponytail reaches the middle of her back now.

"How was your trip, sweetie?" Mrs. Park smiles at me in the rearview mirror.

"Great." Mrs. Park is the type of mom who asks a bunch of questions but actually listens to your answers and remembers what you said later. I missed sitting in their kitchen, chatting, and getting to sample new menu items for the Parks' Korean restaurant while we were away.

"Did everyone stay healthy?"

"Yeah." I fill her in on Mama's rules about tap water and street food, and how we managed to avoid getting sick the whole time. The worst thing I experienced was heat rash, tiny bumps on my skin that itched at night, along with a handful of mosquito bites.

"How's your uncle doing? Better?"

"He's fine, thanks." Thaya Jaan met all of our friends when he was visiting, and he ended up spending a lot of time with Soojin's parents when their church offered to host our Islamic Center's carnival after the center was vandalized. Mr. and Mrs. Park were concerned when Thaya Jaan got sick in the spring and mailed him a get-well card.

"He said to send you his regards," I add.

"Remember how nervous we were when we went to orientation last year?" Soojin changes the subject to school. "Seventh grade is so much more chill already."

"Yeah."

"I hope we have lots of classes together."

"Me too."

I wait for Soojin to ask me more about my trip, but she continues to chatter about what she's heard about the "sneak peek" we're going to and the best seventh-grade teachers according to former students. I recognize one of the names from when Mustafa had her a few years ago.

We pull up to Greendale Middle School, which is no longer intimidating like the beginning of last year, when I worried about getting lost in the halls or forgetting my locker combination. But seeing the brick building makes it official: Summer is over, and this is where I'm going to spend most of my life for the next nine months.

Soojin and I separate to meet our homeroom teachers, pick up our schedules, and find our lockers. While I'm searching for mine, I spot Emily fumbling with her combination a few lockers away and call out to her.

"Hey! Emily!"

"Amina!" Emily grins and then runs over and grabs me. "It felt like you were gone forever!"

She looks so happy to see me, it's hard to believe that there was ever a time when I didn't like her. In less than a year, we've become super close, and Emily is now somebody I trust completely and count as one of my best friends.

"Who do you have?" I ask.

We're comparing our schedules when Soojin finds us, and the three of us discover that we all only have lunch and Spanish together.

"That stinks." Soojin's face falls.

"We're in the same math, you and I, with the teacher you said everyone loves," I point out. "And you and Emily have science, too." That means neither of them will be in my history class this year. Since we've met, Soojin's always been with me in social studies.

"Can you go to Kopp's when we're done?" Emily asks. "My dad says he'll drop you both home."

"Sure," Soojin and I say in unison. Kopp's is Milwaukee's famous, and our favorite, frozen custard place, and we started off the summer with some on the last day of school. It's the perfect way to end the summer too.

The ride with Mr. Heller to Kopp's is quick, and he starts to ask me about Pakistan. But then he gets a work call and stays in the car to have a meeting while we get our custard. I pick my new favorite flavor, peanut butter and chocolate. Zohra loved the Reese's Peanut Butter Cups I took to Pakistan with me, and I'm definitely going to have her try this when she visits. When we look for a shady spot outside to sit down, Soojin notices my bangles.

"Those are pretty," she says, touching them.

"My cousin gave them to me. She has the same ones."

"Nice."

The gifts I bought my friends in Anarkali are sitting in my backpack, and I wait until we are settled on a bench and my custard is safely resting next to me before opening it up.

"Here." I hand them the packages, which are wrapped in Bubble Wrap and Urdu newspaper. "I got you these." I watch their faces as they open them.

"Ooh." Soojin lights up as she sees the green-and-gold box I picked out for her. "This is so beautiful!"

"Thank you, Amina," Emily coos over her turquoise box. "I love it."

"They're handmade in Kashmir," I volunteer, but can guess from my friends' polite nods that they don't know where that is. "I got them at this crowded market where I had to pretend I didn't like anything."

"Why?" Emily asks.

"Because otherwise the price would go up. It's fun to bargain, although I'm not good at it. The market is so crowded. I drank pomegranate juice that someone squeezed right in front of us." My memories pour out of my mouth like the fresh juice flowing from the machine's spout.

"That's so cool," Soojin says as she carefully rewraps her

box in the paper. "It sounds like how my parents describe the markets they used to go to in Korea."

"Have you ever gone back?" I ask, surprised that I don't already know this about her. I don't remember her visiting Korea in all the years we've been friends.

"Not since I moved here when I was four."

"I miss it," I sigh.

"The market?" Emily asks.

"Everything about Pakistan. And especially my cousin."

"I know. I miss my friends from camp so much too," Emily commiserates. "I have to wait a whole year to see them next summer."

I fall silent, trying not to think about how lucky she is. I don't know when I'll go back to Pakistan or get to see my family again. It would be so much easier if I knew it was next year. The night before we left, when I asked Mama to honestly tell me when she thought we might return, she gave me a "we'll see." That's her favorite way to put off answering.

"It's very expensive, Amina," Mama added when she saw my disappointment. "And Baba and I had to take a lot of time off work for this trip. But, insha'Allah, we'll come again in a few years."

A few years.

This trip was after eight years. And even if we keep our promise to everyone to come again sooner, it could be another four or five years. I hope not.

I tune back in to listen to Emily talking about her best friend at camp, who lives in Lansing, Michigan.

"We always do everything together. Next year we're going to be junior counselors."

Soojin shares a few details from her summer of swim team practices and meets, taking a vacation to a lake house with some of her cousins who were visiting from California, and helping out with her parents' food truck.

"I missed your restaurant while I was there," I say. "Everything there was so fresh and delicious, but I got sick of Pakistani food sometimes. My favorite thing was—"

"Me too!" Emily interrupts. "Camp food is so boring! I couldn't wait for the packages my mom would send with snacks."

"My mom's on a healthy breakfast mission," Soojin shares. "She said she's not letting us have cereal before school this year. It has to be oatmeal or eggs or something like that."

"Eww, I hate eggs," Emily groans.

I want to tell my friends so much more about my trip, but my turn to share already seems over. And apart from the handful of photos and silly videos I sent them while I was on the trip, they don't know about everything else that happened. All the memories, funny moments, and unforgettable scenes living inside me, things I've been thinking about and writing about in my notebook, are parts of me that they know nothing about.

It's like I'm a different person, and they have no idea.

How am I supposed to keep my promise to Thaya Jaan and share how wonderful Pakistan is if people aren't interested?

11

Everyone in the community hall claps as Imam Malik takes the stage. I settle into my chair to listen, smooth out the kameez I'm wearing, and fix the scarf on my head.

Imam Malik stands behind a podium that has a sign with the Islamic Center's logo on it and greets us all.

"Assalaamualaikum, dear brothers and sisters. I'm thrilled to see a packed house tonight."

Now that we're full of food from the buffet, everyone knows what's coming next: speeches asking for money. Mustafa has already whipped his phone out under the table and is probably playing a game with Yusuf. Rabiya is sitting next to me, but although we were whispering during the announcements, I make sure to give Imam Malik my attention now.

"I know we ask a lot of you as a community, but you never fail to turn out and support our center, and all those who benefit from it," Imam Malik continues. "And for that I thank Allah for each of you and your generosity."

I've heard a lot of these types of speeches before and can tell that Imam Malik doesn't enjoy giving them. His voice sounds strained, and his easy smile seems forced. Or maybe I'm looking for that because he told me that fundraising is his least favorite part of his job. Plus, he's had to do more of it than usual over the past year, because of the costs of rebuilding the center.

As he continues to speak, I watch Imam Malik clench and unclench his fists and remember how stunned I was to hear that someone as cool and funny as him struggles with speaking in front of people, like I do. His confession and encouragement are what got me through the Quran competition last year and gave me the guts to stand on the stage at the carnival that followed.

Something flutters inside me as I think about that chilly November day, facing hundreds of people, including my family, friends, and community members, and singing my guts out. It was the very first time I'd ever sung a solo in public, and my leg was shaking at first, but once I powered through it like Imam Malik taught me to, I felt electric. It was like something else took over my body as the words forced their way out of my lungs.

When I was done, the applause and cheers were overwhelming. For weeks after it was over, people who I'd never talked to before at school stopped me in the halls to say how beautiful my voice is. It was a little embarrassing, since Rabiya and Soojin were the only ones who ever said stuff like that to me before. But it also felt so nice that it made me want to sing for an audience again. And I didn't care when Mustafa told me my head wouldn't fit through the door anymore if it kept growing bigger from all the compliments.

Imam Malik asks someone to dim the lights, and he shows us a few slides with charts and graphs of budgets, which I tune out. But then he puts up images of people I don't recognize and talks about them.

"We have a number of families who are moving to our community from different countries, including Pakistan, Afghanistan, and the Democratic Republic of the Congo. The Islamic Center has a couple of programs to help support refugees. This includes the apartment setups and welcome dinners that some of you already support."

Rabiya pokes me and points as slides of Mama, Salma Auntie, and their other friends carrying pillows and groceries into different apartments flash onto the screen. A few people in the audience clap for them, and Mama starts to blush. She doesn't like to get attention for the work she does.

Imam Malik continues to explain that they want to expand services beyond the welcoming of families, to include English classes, job training, tutoring, and more.

"But all of this will require more of your efforts and support. So please, be as generous as I know you can be, with your time, talent, and your treasure, insha'Allah."

As Imam Malik explains how people can join various

committees, a few volunteers pass around sign-up sheets and donation envelopes, and waiters bring out plates of baklava, flaky pastry with nuts soaked in syrup, along with pots of steaming-hot mint tea.

Everyone claps for Imam Malik, who ducks his head and rushes off the stage to join his family at a table. His daughter, Sumaiya, crawls into his lap as soon as he sits down and plays with his beard. I got to hold her before dinner started, until she squirmed out of my arms and ran away.

"Did you see the thank-you letter that one of the families sent after our last apartment setup?" Salma Auntie asks us. She passes me the plate of baklava, and I help myself to a big piece. "It was so touching."

"It's hard to imagine being forced to start your life over in a strange place, after a major trauma." Baba shakes his head as he drops sugar into his tea. "I'm glad we're doing something to help, but it doesn't seem like enough."

"We have an idea of something else we could do," Mustafa says.

Everyone focuses on him as he continues to speak.

"Yusuf and I were thinking of inviting the refugee kids to join our basketball team at the center," he continues.

"Won't you have too many players then?" I ask.

"Well, some new kids might need time to learn how to play, so we could form a practice team. We thought we'd combine basketball with tutoring in English. We'll get our friends to be tutors and coaches for service hours."

Hamid Uncle thumps Mustafa on the back.

"Masha'Allah! What a great idea. I'm so proud of you both."

"Thanks, Uncle," Mustafa says. I have to admit, it's been impressive to see my brother turn into a coach to the younger boys at the center, who all adore him. Even tonight, one of the dads with a kid on the team was raving about Mustafa and his coaching style to Baba, who was bursting with pride. It doesn't even matter that his team lost most of their games and didn't make the playoffs.

"What about you girls?" Salma Auntie asks Rabiya and me.

"What?" Rabiya asks.

"What are you going to do to help? You heard the imam. Everyone needs to chip in."

"Amina and I are making Eid cards and selling them, and we'll give the money to the center," Rabiya replies.

I stare at Rabiya. This is the first I've heard about this.

"Right, Amina?" Rabiya's big eyes are wide, and she nods her head slowly.

"Um yeah, I guess," I say. Rabiya should know by now that art is not my thing. I can barely draw a stick figure.

When the grown-ups all start talking among themselves, I whisper to her.

"Why'd you say that? You know I suck at art."

"We can't let the boys beat us. We have to do something too," Rabiya explains. "Plus, we should, right?"

"Yeah."

Everything with Rabiya is a contest, and she never backs down from a challenge. She's the one who pushes me the hardest to sing and tries to get me to put up YouTube videos of myself performing because she says I'm better than other people doing it. She stands up to the boys if they aren't nice to us and convinces our parents to let us have sleepovers. I know if I told her about my attempts to write a song, she would hound me until I shared them with her.

I think of the last jumbled lyrics that I scribbled into my notebook, words and phrases like "where is your heart," "missing you," "are you home now," and "the other half of me."

"They do, kind of. Right?" Rabiya says.

"What?"

"I said, those people in that picture are just like your family. Why are you so spaced out?" I hear impatience in her voice.

Photos from the apartment setups and different families are rotating on the screen, and Rabiya points to one with a mother, father, and three kids when it comes up again.

"Well, maybe the older two kids," I say.

There are three kids in the photo of a refugee family, but two of them could be about Mustafa's and my ages. They aren't smiling in the photo, though, and their eyes are dark and serious. The image of the little boy in the market in Pakistan comes to mind, and guilt over all of the extra food in my stomach makes it churn.

I wonder what terrible things forced this family to leave their home forever and escape to a new place where they don't fit in or speak the language fluently. Now maybe people will look at them funny, speak for them, or act confused when they try, like when I speak Urdu.

Imam Malik and Rabiya are right—we should all do something to help. We'd need other people to do the same thing for us if we were ever in that kind of terrible situation. But no matter how pushy Rabiya can be, I don't want to make Eid cards, and I doubt anyone would buy them if I did. I'd rather find something I can do on my own to help out, in my own way. I just have to figure out what that is.

12

It's fourth period. I've met my teachers, gotten a syllabus, heard about classroom rules, and done things like play get-to-know-you bingo in each class I've had so far. Now that I'm in history, I settle in for more of the same first-day-of-school business.

"Ah-MEE-nah?" Mr. Griffiths calls out.

"AHH-min-ah," I correct for the fourth time today.

"Ahh-meh-nah," Mr. Griffiths mumbles, before moving on to the next name on his list.

I turn to my left, where I'd normally see Soojin sitting and exchange an eye roll with her, but then I remember she isn't in my history class this year. Glancing around the room, I spot a couple of people that I'm sort of friends with, Briana and Jess. Mr. Griffiths has no trouble saying their names, and when they notice me, they acknowledge me with friendly waves.

When he gets through attendance, Mr. Griffiths talks about his goals and expectations for the year. He uses phrases like "mutual respect" and "exemplary manners," while people slump in their seats and yawn, waiting for practical information like grading or homework policies.

Finally, after what seems like half the class, Mr. Griffiths stops talking and hands out stacks of papers for us to pass around. I expect another syllabus but am surprised to see it's called Living Wax Museum.

An assignment on the first day of school?

"Our major project this quarter is an interactive learning initiative. Over the next nine weeks you will become an expert on an individual from history, learning enough to become that person and assume their identity."

Someone in the back makes a crack about identity theft.

"I'm not talking about breaking the law," Mr. Griffiths

continues, not appearing the slightest bit amused. "You're going to pretend to be someone important in history—a warrior, artist, inventor, leader, or writer—anyone you want. You will research this person extensively, through memoir, biography, and other sources, and then capture the voice of the person. We will be doing a series of research activities around the person, writing, peer editing, and more."

The guy sitting behind me groans and mutters about how much he hates writing and thought this was history class, but Mr. Griffiths ignores him and keeps speaking.

"For now, you need to start thinking about the person you want to select. It can be anyone, as long as they have made a significant and positive contribution to history or society in some way."

Justin, dressed in a jersey like usual, raises his hand.

"Can it be an athlete?" he asks.

"Not if the person's primary achievement is playing a sport. But if you can make a case for their significant contribution to history, like through activism or humanitarian works, then maybe."

"Yes!" Justin pumps his fist in celebration, and I wonder who his athlete is. I still find it hard to believe that Emily had a crush on Justin last year, although that fizzled out pretty quickly once he found out about it.

"What about a famous criminal?" a girl named Abigail asks, and I stop thinking about Justin and Emily and how I blurted out her secret last year and almost ruined the chance to be friends with her. Lucky for me, she believed it was an accident—which it honestly was.

Mr. Griffiths shakes his head. "I said a positive contribution to history or society."

"What if it's a criminal who helps society?" she presses. "Like Robin Hood?"

"Robin Hood is fictional," Mr. Griffiths sighs. "You need to research real people, and people who you can find a sufficient amount of material about."

The questions continue until the end of the period, and Mr. Griffiths seems relieved when the bell rings and stops his last answer midsentence as everyone jumps out of their seats. He goes to his desk and takes a gulp from the travel coffee mug sitting there. I didn't need to ask any questions, because I've already decided which person I want to pick.

I find Soojin and Emily in the corner of the cafeteria, at the same table we claimed as ours last year. It started off with Soojin and me at the beginning of sixth grade, until Emily joined us. By the end of the year Allison and Margot were sitting with us regularly too.

"Hey, Amina. Look what I have."

Emily holds out her sandwich in my direction, and I peer at the meat squished inside the bread.

"Is that a . . . shami kabob?" I can't hide my amazement. Emily used to act scared of Pakistani and Korean food before she became friends with Soojin and me.

Emily laughs. "We ran out of the ones we had in the freezer, but this lady makes them and sells them, so we got a bunch more from her."

I don't know what is more surprising, the fact that Emily's family is buying food from an auntie, or that she's eating something I banned my mother from putting in my lunch when I was in second grade. I insisted on "regular" lunch foods like peanut butter.

"They're so good. Want some?" She holds out the other half of her sandwich for me.

I take a small bite, and the ground mincemeat patty is exactly the way I like it, not too spicy, and no big pieces of onion or coriander.

"Yum." I hand the sandwich back to Emily. "I'm going to ask my mom if she can order some. She says they're too much work to make."

The turkey sandwich I made last night sits in front of me, and it suddenly seems boring. I never thought I'd actually miss eating Pakistani food for lunch. But now that I haven't been, it's become one of the many things I miss about Pakistan every day.

"Are you feeling okay?" Emily reaches her hand out across the table.

"Yeah, I'm okay," I mumble, and look down. I can't explain the crush of feelings that are squeezing my insides, so I don't try.

Emily's half sandwich appears on my lunch mat.

"You have this. We have more at home." She smiles when I look up.

"Oh, thank you." I'm touched by the gesture and accept it gratefully. "Take my turkey."

After I polish off the rest of the kabob, I tell my friends, "I just had history," remembering what I was excited to share with them. "And we have to do this big Living Wax Museum project."

"Everyone does," Soojin says. "In the whole grade. I'm thinking of being Ada Lovelace."

"Who?" I ask.

"She was a computer programmer. I have a book about her that my dad got me. I think he's trying to inspire me to work with computers instead of animals," she laughs. Soojin has wanted to be a veterinarian for as long as I can remember.

"What's this project?" Emily asks.

"You'll hear about it when you have history," I explain. "You have to research someone and then act like them."

"It's kind of like being in a show," Allison adds. "My

family went when my sister did it, and everyone in her class was standing frozen, like statues in a wax museum. We pushed a button, and they came to life and told us about themselves, and we asked questions."

"So, it's like acting?" Emily looks worried. "Because I can't act."

"I mean, a little," Allison continues. "It's like giving an oral report, but you're wearing a costume. My sister was Jane Austen, so she spoke in a really bad British accent and watched *Pride and Prejudice* like fifty times to practice it. I was so glad when it was finally over."

"Do you know who you want to be?" Soojin asks me.

"Malala Yousafzai."

"You mean like *Malala* Malala?"

"Yeah, that Malala. That's her full name."

"Isn't she alive? I think you have to pick someone dead."

"Mr. Griffiths only said someone who has changed history, and Malala definitely did. She was the youngest person to ever win the Nobel Peace Prize. And she's from Pakistan." I can't hide the pride in my voice.

"Well, I would check to make sure. It's like most of your grade for the quarter," Soojin warns, and I can't help but notice that she seems more interested in the rules than in how amazing Malala is.

"I will," I say. But Malala is definitely a part of history, and an important person who shares my background. I know there is a ton of information about her, and I'm sure I can find out more from Thaya Jaan and Zohra. Dressing like her won't be any problem at all either. And I can already imitate a Pakistani accent pretty well too. I can't imagine why Malala isn't the perfect choice.

13

My last class of the day is my favorite, chorus with Ms. Holly. She lights up as I walk through the door.

"Amina! How was your summer?"

"Really fun. I went to Pakistan."

"Oh, that's right! I want to hear all about it." Ms. Holly smiles, and I remember I wanted to share the qawali music I've been listening to with her, including Nusrat Fateh Ali Khan and the Sabri Brothers. I'm certain she'll fall in love with the drums and harmonium, the chorus and the clapping, and the way it sounds like nothing else out there. But for now, I settle into my seat.

The room is filled with many of the same people who

were in my class last year, with the notable exception of Soojin. She signed up for dance this year. And instead of the eighth graders, who've moved on to high school, we have a crop of sixth graders who seem as uncertain as I must have been last year.

Ms. Holly takes attendance, goes over class procedures, and talks about how we'll soon be preparing for this year's winter choral concert. My palms start to sweat thinking about the one last year, where I played the piano and then sang my first solo. This time my clammy hands aren't because of nerves but excitement—or maybe a little of both.

Ms. Holly, along with Soojin, was someone who pushed me to sign up for a solo from the start. After I refused, she gave me songs to practice at home in case I changed my mind. At the time, I never thought I would, but it was as if Ms. Holly could read my mind and knew that I was secretly wishing I had the guts to do it all along. I'm definitely going to sing again this winter.

"I hope that many of you will join the drama club I run." Ms. Holly glances at me and then continues to speak to the room. "We meet once a week after school, sometimes more when we are close to a performance. We're going to experiment with a bunch of new types of shows this year, like a one-act play and a spring musical and maybe an open-mic night."

A kid I've never seen before with long brown hair that hangs over one of his eyes raises his hand.

"What about the production?" he asks.

"What do you mean, uh . . . is it Nico?

"Yeah," Nico replies. "Who handles audio tech for the shows?"

"Me, mostly. I pick the arrangements, and some of the teachers volunteer for shows," Ms. Holly explains.

"Do you need help?" Nico pushes his hair out of his face and sinks farther into his seat.

"Sure! I'd welcome that. Why don't you come to our first club meeting next week and we can discuss?" Ms. Holly smiles warmly, and Nico nods his head ever so slightly.

I'm curious to know what Nico is talking about, but as the bell rings, he crouches behind his desk and rummages through his backpack. I pause for a moment but then leave to catch up with Soojin and Emily at our lockers before I head to the bus line.

"Hey. I think I'm going to join the drama club," I say when I see them. "Will you do it with me?"

"Don't they put on plays?" Emily frowns. "I told you before, I can't act."

"Not just plays. Ms. Holly says it's different types of singing and performing. Come on, it'll be more fun with you."

"I'm signing up for chess club. My mom's making me. She says it's important for critical thinking or something."

We all nod in sympathy. Emily's mom is a lawyer, and it seems like she wins all the arguments in their family. I remember when Baba was pushing Mustafa to play chess or join quiz bowl, instead of basketball. Now that Mustafa is both playing and coaching basketball, and getting high enough grades, Baba's a bit more relaxed. Plus, since we've been back from our trip, Mustafa's been extra good, which I know is so our parents will take him driving. He got his learner's permit before we left for Pakistan and is desperate to practice enough to get his license as soon as he's allowed.

"What about you and drama club?" I turn to Soojin hopefully.

"I'm thinking of running for student council," Soojin says. "I won't have time for that and my dance lessons and something else after school."

"Oh." Drama club suddenly seems less exciting.

"You should totally do it, though," Soojin encourages. "Especially if it means more singing and stuff. Plus, you love Ms. Holly."

"I guess." Ms. Holly is wonderful, but I'd rather be with my friends.

"We'll still hang out. You should come over soon," Soojin says as we file out of the school.

"Sure," I say. But as I wave bye to my friends and we walk toward our buses, it feels like we're each moving in different directions in other ways too. And I'm still unsure about where exactly I'm heading.

14

In the picture of Malala on the cover of the book, she's smiling in a mysterious *Mona Lisa* kind of way, and her dark eyes are thoughtful. She's wearing a scarf on her head, but there's some hair showing in the front, like Thayee wears hers when she goes out, and she has bangles on her wrist like me.

"What are you reading?" Baba stops as he walks by where I'm curled up on the couch with a fuzzy blanket and peeks over my shoulder.

"A book about Malala. For my project."

"You didn't waste any time, did you?" Baba's eyes crinkle in the corners, like Thaya Jaan's. Now that Baba is getting more gray in his hair, he's starting to resemble his older brother more than he used to.

"They had this at my library at school."

"Good for you. The world should listen to young people more." Baba bends down and kisses the top of my head, as if he's sending his little piece of wisdom directly into my brain. "Don't you want to sleep? It's late, and you had a long week at school."

"It's Friday. I can't go to bed yet. And I'm waiting for it to get late enough to call Zohra."

Baba pulls his phone out of his pocket and checks it. "It's eight in the morning over there. I think it's fine to call now."

"Okay." I jump off the sofa and take the tablet he offers me while Baba goes to the other couch and turns on the TV with the volume low. I don't mind that he sometimes listens in on my conversations with Zohra because I know he likes to hear about what's going on with everyone in Lahore as much as I do.

For a change, Zohra picks up right away.

"Salaams," she says while she's looking in the other direction and mouthing something to someone else.

"Salaams! What are you doing?"

"Nothing. How about you?"

"I was reading about Malala."

"Malala? What for?" Zohra's eyes are darting around the room instead of focusing on me.

"I'm going to do a big project at school on her. I'll have to research her life and her impact on history, and then I'm going to write essays and make presentations to my class. And then at the end I'm going to dress up like her and pretend to be her for a special show with everyone's families and the whole school."

I say everything quickly and then remember that Zohra sometimes has trouble following me if I speak too fast. That must be the reason she's not concentrating on the screen.

"That's nice." Zohra looks back at the camera and gives me a smile, but it doesn't reach her eyes.

Something is wrong.

"What's going on?" I ask.

Zohra glances to her left again and nods her head at someone else in the room.

"Nothing," she says.

"Zohra," I press. "What's the matter? Who's there with you?"

"It's Ammi," she says, and flips the camera so I can see the profile of Thayee talking on the phone. "Sorry. You were telling me something?"

"Yeah. About my project."

"Right. Malala." Zohra nods at me this time. "Go on."

"That's it. I thought maybe you could tell me more about her since she's from Pakistan."

"Oh." Zohra pauses. "I don't know that much about her."

"Okay." Something is definitely up with Zohra. Normally she would get animated and start spilling any random facts that she knows about Malala. She loves to drop knowledge any chance she gets.

I stare at my cousin.

"Zohra," I repeat. "Is everything okay?"

Zohra tries to smile again, but as I watch, her face crumples and she shakes her head slowly.

"What is it?" Dread spreads inside me.

"It's Abu." Zohra bites on her lip. "He fell in the bathroom last night."

"No!" I gasp, as my pulse quickens. "Is Thaya Jaan okay?"

"He got dizzy and fell. He's okay now, but it was scary. Ammi didn't want to worry you all."

Baba is standing over me in an instant, and he takes the tablet.

"When did this happen? Is he home? Did you take him to the doctor?" he asks.

"It was late last night. He's home. His doctor friend came over and checked him right away."

Baba shakes his head. "Can you put Bhabi on the line?"

Thayee comes on the phone and says something about how they didn't want us to panic and that Thaya Jaan is doing okay. They're speaking in Urdu, and I get the gist of what they're saying but miss parts of it. Baba asks for his brother, but he's sleeping. Mama comes into the room too and asks a few more questions. And then Baba makes Thayee promise to call later when Thaya Jaan is awake, even if it's three a.m. our time. She agrees, but I bet she isn't going to do it. Grown-ups act like waking someone up at night is a terrible crime.

Baba hangs up the call and sits down on the chair I was in, cradling his head in his hands. Mama pats his back and tries to reassure him.

"It sounds like Bhai Jaan is doing okay. His friend checked him out."

"He's an internist, not a cardiologist. He should get an EKG."

"People get dizzy for so many reasons. He could have gotten up too quickly. Or maybe his blood sugar dropped."

"Maybe." Baba starts to rumple his hair. "What if he's concussed? They shouldn't have let him sleep."

"She didn't say he hit his head. Let's get more details before we panic," Mama says.

"I know, I know—you're right," Baba sighs.

"Is Thaya Jaan going to be okay?" I ask. I was planning to talk to him about my project and hoped to see his slow smile spread across his face, the one reserved for when he's especially pleased about something. I could tell him I was trying to do what he asked of me, by sharing the story of a hero from Pakistan.

"I hope so, geeta," Baba says. The crinkles around his eyes are replaced with worry. "Insha'Allah, he'll be fine."

When Thaya Jaan felt tightness in his chest earlier this year, Baba was super stressed out. He insisted that the doctors in Lahore share all his test results with him, spoke to them on the phone daily, and almost seemed to be managing everything from over here. I'd never seen him so tense and worried, and he almost flew over there when Thaya Jaan had to have a procedure to look inside his heart and put in a balloon to open up a clogged artery. But Thaya Jaan stopped him and said to come with the rest of us when he was better, which is why we visited in the summer.

I was scared back then too, and as I think of the helplessness on Zohra's face, there's a hammering in my chest.

"Insha'Allah, he'll be fine," I repeat to myself, but it doesn't stop the fear growing inside me.

15

"So, I decided to run for class president," Soojin declares confidently, and then peers at me, waiting for my reaction. I stop moving the rusted swing we're sitting on together on her patio and turn to face her.

"President?" I repeat. "That's big."

"I know."

"You sure you don't want to start with treasurer? To see if you even like student council first?"

"I thought about that." Soojin shrugs and twists one of the rings on her fingers. "But I don't want to be treasurer. I want to be president."

"Really?" I'm not trying to argue with her. It's just that

student council is something Soojin's never mentioned before this school year, and I don't know why she's into it all of a sudden.

Soojin jumps off the swing and starts to quickly pace in front of me as she speaks. I'm drowsy from sitting in the sun, after eating a plateful of leftover kimchi fried rice from Soojin's fridge for a snack after school. And although we promised to do our homework before I leave, we've only been hanging out and talking so far. It feels nice, though, since we haven't done this in forever.

"Nathan was president last year, and he didn't have another position before he ran," Soojin says. "I thought about trying for secretary, but why should I limit myself when I have a shot at president?"

"I guess. But why do you want to do it at all?" I pause, and then try to clarify my question so it doesn't sound like criticism. "I mean, does that sound fun to you?"

Soojin sighs and shakes her head. When she speaks again, it's like she's explaining something basic to a little kid.

"Amina, you can only make a difference if you get

involved, right? And I want to run in high school, so I need experience."

"I thought you wanted to do the dance team in high school," I say. As long as I can remember, Soojin's been taking private dance lessons and talking about joining the dance team and competing in high school.

"I do." Soojin does a little spin that makes me smile. "But this summer I talked a lot with my cousin who just graduated college. She wants to run for her city council. And she says we can't afford to sit on the sidelines because we're the next generation of leaders."

"I guess." It sounds like Soojin had a lot to think about this summer too.

"Plus, it looks good for college," Soojin adds.

"College?" Soojin reminds me of Mustafa, when he was trying to convince Baba last year that being on the basketball team was important to show he was a well-rounded person on his college applications. "Isn't that kind of far away?"

"Not that far, Amina. We'll be applying in like only four

years." Soojin leans over and starts to pick leaves out of one of the flowerpots with dead flowers in it.

That's so Soojin. She's already planning for four years from now. But I'm not ready to think about high school yet.

"You should do it," I finally say. "If it's what you want, you should go for it."

"I'm going to. But I need help with my campaign." Soojin stands up and brushes the dirt off her hands. "Will you be my campaign manager?"

"Sure. But don't most people just vote for their friends?" I ask. I don't mention that Nathan probably won because he's one of the most popular kids in the grade, not because he had the funniest posters or because he handed out stickers with his face on them.

"Sometimes. I'll just have to convince enough people to vote for me."

"What if you don't win?" I ask, thinking about what would hold me back from running in the first place. It would be humiliating to put in all that effort, just to find out it wasn't enough.

"Then I'll try again next year." Soojin sets her jaw and looks determined.

"What are you going to promise?" I ask.

"What do you mean?"

"Don't people who run for student council promise things, to get you to vote for them?"

Soojin faces me and stands extra tall and even straighter than usual.

"I'll promise to be honest, and to work hard, and to listen to what everyone has to say," she lists, as if she's already thought about her answer.

I don't have the heart to tell her those are the same things everyone says every year. If I'm not going to fail as campaign manager, we'll have to think of something better.

"Girls?" Mrs. Park calls from the kitchen window. "Don't you want to do your homework? Amina, can you stay for dinner?"

"We will," Soojin replies.

"I'll ask my mom," I answer as I text Mama, hoping she'll say yes. I'm still comfortably full of the rice, but whatever

Mrs. Park is cooking inside smells delicious. And even though there hasn't been any news about Thaya Jaan, Baba's been on edge and anxious about him all week. He's all we seem to talk about at dinner, which makes me nervous too.

"What about you and drama club?" Soojin asks. "Are you going to do it?"

"I think so." Listening to Soojin talk about the future makes me realize I probably need to do something, and the club did sound like it could be fun—as long as there's more singing and less drama in it.

"Is everyone from chorus joining?"

"Julie is. And I heard a few others in class say they were coming. And I think that new kid Nico is interested."

"The guy with the long hair?"

"Yeah."

"He's in my gym class. He barely talks to anyone," Soojin says.

"He probably doesn't know anybody." I think about what it would be like to start seventh grade in a new middle school and can imagine acting the same way.

"I'll make sure to ask him to vote for me before anyone else does," Soojin says as she does another little spin and then bows before me with her arms spread out.

As I watch my friend, something in the way Soojin looks so sure of herself impresses me. It's like she's ready for a bigger stage than before. I hope that other people will believe in her as much as I do. And it wouldn't hurt to have some of her confidence rub off on me.

16

Ms. Holly's voice echoes from where we're sitting on the stage in a circle. The empty auditorium is dark and spooky with the main lights off, but the stage lights are shining on us. As we wrap up, we're discussing one-act plays.

"I think we should do *The Hundred Dresses*. My friend did that at her school and said it was amazing," Julie says.

"If she just did it, shouldn't we be original?" a girl named Natasha argues.

"That was like two years ago. And she goes to a private school all the way in River Hills. It's totally fine if we do the same thing." Julie speaks with the air of someone who isn't accustomed to being challenged. And somehow, I've noticed, that has prevented people from trying for as long as I've known her.

I haven't made any suggestions, since I'm not exactly sure what a one-act play is, or what I'm doing here. In addition to Julie, most of the other kids are people I don't know or hang out with. I've been staying in the back, keeping to myself and listening, and trying to decide if this club is a good fit for me after all.

Maybe they won't notice if I don't come back next week.

"Let's think about it and take votes next time we meet," Ms. Holly says. "Do a little research in the meantime and see what other choices you come up with."

Everyone immediately whips out their phones to "do a little research." I have no idea what to search for, so I look around and notice that Nico, the new boy from chorus, has a laptop open on his legs. He slips on some headphones and starts tapping on the keys.

When a bunch of bright digital boxes light up his screen, I can't help but peek at it. A series of lines form waves in green and black. I've never seen anything like it.

"What's that?" I surprise myself by inching closer to Nico and pointing toward his computer.

Nico slips off one side of his headphones and tilts his head toward me.

"What is that?" I repeat.

"A digital audio workstation."

"What are you doing?"

"Making a beat." Nico takes off his headphones and hands them to me, and I slip them on. He presses a key, and I hear a mix of keyboard and drums that's simple but catchy.

"You did this? All by yourself?"

"Yeah." Nico nods slightly, and I notice flecks of gray in his brown eyes.

"How?"

"It's pretty easy. You open the synthesizer and record a melody. Then you add background chords and harmonies. And then you mix in other instruments." Nico pauses after each sentence, as if to check that I'm still listening. He tries to tuck his hair behind his ears, but it's not quite long enough and flops out again.

"It sounds great," I say.

"Thanks," Nico mumbles. "I'm not finished."

"How do you add the other instruments?"

"With plug-ins, like for guitar or piano. Or you can use a sampler."

"What's a sampler?" I can't tell if Nico is finding all my questions annoying. But as long as he keeps answering, I want to know.

"Basically, someone went into a recording studio and played all the notes from a real instrument and made a digital file for all of them. Each note is a sample that you can arrange the way you want by using the keyboard."

Nico opens another box and starts to demonstrate by playing "Mary Had a Little Lamb" using the keyboard, and it sounds exactly like a saxophone.

"See? It's pretty simple."

"That's awesome." I reach over and press a note. "How'd you learn to do all this?"

"My uncle gave me his old laptop when he got a new one. It already had this studio software on it, so he showed me a few things, and I've been teaching myself."

"Wow. And I'm writing songs on paper," I say, half to myself.

"You write songs?" Nico's eyes grow wider, and he instantly seems more comfortable with me.

"Kind of. I mean, not exactly. But Ms. Holly pushed me to start composing, and she gave me blank sheet music last year. I still have it."

"Well, I can help you enter the digital era," Nico offers, and then holds out his hand.

I stare at him, confused.

Does he want me to hold his hand?

Nico glances at his headphones, which are around my neck. My cheeks flush as I take them off, hand them to him, and pray he doesn't notice.

"If you want," Nico quickly adds. His skin is pale, and the tip of his ear turns red as he tries to tuck his hair behind it again.

"What?"

"I'll show you how to do it if you want."

"Oh, okay." I've played around on my piano and come up with some original stuff, but mostly simple melodies. The thought of turning my ideas into an actual song, with a melody and harmonies, and the lyrics I've been working on, sounds exactly like what I've been dreaming about for weeks now.

"Amina!" A harsh voice jars me out of my thoughts.

Mustafa is standing in the shadows of the auditorium seats, glaring at me.

"What are you doing? Mom and I have been waiting outside for like ten minutes. Come on already!"

I jump up, mumble bye to Nico, and notice that while we were engrossed in his laptop, almost everyone else left, except for Julie and Ms. Holly, who are talking in the corner.

"Who's the kid?" Mustafa asks after I've grabbed my backpack and we're in the hallway heading out of school to where Mama's parked the car.

"Some guy. I don't know him," I say as casually as possible.

"You seemed pretty cozy for strangers." Mustafa studies my face.

"He was showing me something," I say, and get into the backseat of the car. It's true that I don't know Nico. But it's also true that I want to. Not in the way Mustafa is implying, though. I want him to show me how to finally bring the music that lives inside me to life.

17

"What do you mean you're not going?" Soojin waves her drink around, and I'm afraid it's going to splash on me. "You have to go."

"Why?" I shrug and pull out the granola bar in my lunch. "We didn't last year."

"That was sixth grade, Amina. Everyone goes to the dances in seventh grade. You have to come."

"Really?" I can't help but wonder if this is like Soojin deciding she wanted to start carrying a purse last year and insisting that I needed to join her. I quickly gave up on using one after I left mine in science and math on the same day.

"Everyone goes." Emily is solemn as she bites into her

sandwich, which I noticed is kabob free today. "She's right."

"Plus, if I'm running for class president, I have to prove that I have school spirit, and I can't do that if I don't show up," Soojin adds. "You said you'd help me, right?"

"Yeah."

"So I want to hand out stickers or pencils at the dance."

"At the dance? What are people going to do with them?" I imagine her campaign merchandise strewn across the floor of the cafeteria and kids stepping on it in their fancy shoes.

"You don't want your stuff wasted," Emily agrees.

"True." Soojin pauses to consider what we're saying. "Maybe I should just put up posters outside?"

"Or maybe we can go and have fun. And do the campaign stuff later," Emily says. "When people are paying attention."

"I guess." Soojin's lower lip sticks out like it does when she's thinking hard. "I want to win, though. I think Julie is running against me."

"We'll help you," I assure her. "You can win."

"Okay, but you have to come to the dance," Soojin insists.

"I'll ask. What are you going to wear?"

"I have that dress from my aunt's shower. The baby-blue one. Remember?" Soojin pulls up a photo on her phone and shows us.

"You looked so good," I say. Soojin reminds me of a ballerina in the dress. "What about you, Emily?"

"I bet my mom is going to want to pick something for me. She's been waiting my whole life for me to go to dances. She made such a big deal about fifth-grade promotion. I was the only kid wearing a fancy white dress," Emily groans.

My mom is exactly the opposite of Emily's. I'm 100 percent certain she has not been waiting for me to go to dances, and I wonder what she'll say when I ask. I remember Mustafa getting a ton of questions about going to homecoming last year, even though he was going without a date. I was hoping I wouldn't have to think about any of this until next year.

"What about you, Amina?" Emily asks.

"What?"

"What are you wearing?"

"Well, if I go—"

"You have to go!" Soojin interrupts.

"If I'm allowed to go, I have no idea." I frown.

If getting Mama to agree on the shirt I'm wearing right now was a challenge, picking out something to wear to a school dance will be a nightmare. And nothing in my closet is going to work. The last dress I wore was a long, thick, striped sweater dress from winter that would be too warm.

"You'll be allowed," Soojin says with confidence. I hope she's right. I think.

"So, do people actually dance at the dances?" I ask.

"Of course," Emily says. "There's a DJ and everything."

"Oh."

"Or do you mean like slow dance?" Soojin watches me closely.

"No. I was just wondering." I stuff some of the granola bar in my mouth.

Soojin slaps her hand on the table, leans in, and whispers, "Are you asking because of that guy?"

I don't answer and keep chewing.

"What guy?" Emily moves closer.

"The new one from drama club. With the hair. What's his name again?"

"Shhhh! No!" I whip my head around to see if anyone is listening.

"Who is he, Amina? I can't believe you didn't tell me." Emily pouts. "I tell you everything."

"There's nothing to tell! Promise. I just talked to him for the first time last week. And he's into making music and said he would show me how."

"Wait—you're making music together?" Soojin holds back a smile.

"Ooh, I bet you make beautiful music together!" Emily adds with a giggle.

"You guys aren't funny," I hiss. But I scan the room again and don't say his name aloud just in case.

Soojin and Emily lock eyes for a second. I know what they're thinking, but they're wrong. Why is my talking to Nico making everyone freak out? Is it because Emily had a crush on Justin since last year, and it became a big deal when

I told Bradley by mistake? Or because Soojin changes her mind about who she thinks she likes every few months? It's like they're desperately waiting for me to like someone too.

But maybe I want to be friends with a boy without everyone assuming he's my boyfriend. And why do they have to be a million times more interested in Nico than when I talk about Zohra or tell them things about Pakistan?

I decide to ignore them and let them have their fun.

Nico is only a friend. Actually, he's not even a friend yet. And it doesn't mean anything to think about someone who's a friend, or almost a friend.

Or does it?

18

"Why is Baba on the phone with doctors again? Is Thaya Jaan okay?" I ask Mama when I get home from school. She's scrubbing the counters that already seem clean, which is a clue that she's stressed out.

"The doctors are trying to figure out what's going on."

"What do you mean 'figure out'? Why don't they know yet?"

Mama pushes the hair off her forehead with the back of her rubber-gloved hand.

"They're running a bunch of tests and trying to determine why he's been getting dizzy. But they're pretty sure it's his heart again."

I grip the edge of the counter. Hearing bad news about Thaya Jaan makes my knees start to buckle, like they might stop working to keep my legs straight. Mama watches me, sighs, and takes off her gloves.

"Come. Sit." She motions to the table, so I follow orders and sit down. "Want some milk?"

"Okay."

Mama pours me a glass, and then takes a package of cookies from the pantry, the ones we brought back from Pakistan, and hands it to me.

I take a sip of the milk and tear open the package. They're the double-chocolate sandwich cookies I love, delicious but not super sweet. The best part about them is the giant granules of sugar sprinkled on top.

"I know you're worried," Mama says. "We all are."

I nod with my mouth full.

"Baba is talking to his doctors every day, and the important thing is that Thaya Jaan isn't in the hospital."

"What about the hospital?" Mustafa walks into the kitchen and opens up the refrigerator.

"Nothing. No one is in the hospital, and, insha'Allah, it stays that way."

"Can we go driving today?" Mustafa asks as he pours himself some milk. "I need to practice."

"Maybe Baba can take you when he gets home," Mama says. She always tries to get out of going driving with Mustafa even though he says she's easier to be on the road with than our father.

"Yusuf is having a few friends over for a FIFA tournament this weekend for his birthday. Can I go?" Mustafa stands over the table and grabs some of the cookies with his free hand.

"I think so." Mama doesn't seem to be fully listening, and I can imagine her acting surprised when Mustafa mentions this later.

"And I have a thing at school next Friday," I add.

"What thing?"

"A dance."

"Dance?" Mustafa grins. "The back-to-school dance? I remember those."

"I don't know about a dance." Mama frowns.

"Why not?" Mustafa asks. "I went."

"Did you? In seventh grade?" Now Mama gives Mustafa her full attention.

Mustafa shoves an entire cookie into his mouth at once and washes it down with some milk. "I think so. I definitely went in eighth. Remember?"

"I don't know about this, Amina," Mama starts.

"It's a school event, totally chaperoned. What's wrong with a bunch of kids hanging out in the cafeteria? You have to let her go." Mustafa grabs another cookie, and I want to tell him to stop eating them all, or we'll run out. But I don't.

Mama doesn't respond and seems to be considering what he's saying.

"You don't want her to be socially . . . stunted, do you?" Mustafa adds with a little smirk.

"Okay, enough from you." Mama takes a cookie and bites off a piece. "I could use some chai with this. Can you put on water for me?"

"I need something to wear, too," I mumble.

"Like what?"

"Like a dress or something."

Mama thinks for a moment.

"What about that nice pink shalwar kameez you wore in Pakistan?" She brightens, like it's the best idea she's ever had.

"Mama!" I protest. "You can't be serious."

"It's like a dress. It's got that belt."

"I'm not wearing a shalwar kameez to school!"

"Why not? It's so nice. And it's full sleeve."

I stare at Mustafa with raised eyebrows, silently pleading for help. He shrugs.

"Mama!" I turn back to my mother. "I can't be the only person wearing a shalwar kameez at school. Everyone will think it's weird."

"No one will. They'll love it. I wore one to Baba's holiday party, and all the ladies said it was so elegant and commented on the fabric."

"Yeah, but they're all old."

Mustafa snorts. "True," he says. "She's right. No one wants to be the one sticking out in ethnic clothes at school."

"Fine," Mama sighs, and finishes her bite. "You should be proud of your culture. But okay. We'll find you something."

Mustafa gives me a little salute as he leaves the kitchen. As I realize he helped me win the battle to go to the dance, and not dress like my mom, I'm not convinced that I want to go yet. A moment later he darts back in and grabs the rest of the cookies in the package. I fight him for one and it breaks in half and he lets me have it.

As I savor the last piece from our cookie stash, I think back to our daily chai in Pakistan. I'd give anything to be there right now and to see the tea trolley with unlimited chocolate sandwich cookies, juicy mangos, and even that hot chocolate. Most of all, I want to see Thaya Jaan smiling as he watches all of us together, somehow saying so much with so few words. Like the grandfather I never had the chance to know, he's the glue that connects my life here to my bigger family and all its history and traditions. And now that I feel so close to him, I need Thaya Jaan to remain in my life for a very long time.

19

I raise my hand to go first, but Mr. Griffiths calls on Keira to present her research update to the class.

"I picked Harriet Tubman for my project," she begins.

Imam Malik advised me to go first when I'm speaking in public, so I have less time to get worked up about it. But since I wasn't picked, I study my notes on Malala again and try to stay calm. I'm extra nervous, since this assignment is worth fifty points. Mr. Griffiths told us that he wants to make sure we're making good progress with our research and that we discover any gaps before our big presentations, only four weeks from now.

"Harriet Tubman was an amazing person who led

enslaved people to safety through what became known as the Underground Railroad. When she herself was safe, she returned several times to help others escape to the North," Keira continues.

I watch how Keira makes sure to look up as she reads from her paper and takes deep breaths between sentences like an expert speaker, and I make a mental note to try that. When she finishes, Mr. Griffiths asks about her sources and makes a few suggestions of other places she can check out. Keira seems pleased with herself when he says she's off to a great start and practically skips back to her seat.

I raise my hand again, but Mr. Griffiths calls on Justin next, who saunters up to the front of the room and crinkles the edges of his paper as he starts speaking. His voice is big and projects like he's in a theater, not a classroom.

"I picked Alexander Graham Bell, since he invented the phone. I'm a huge fan of my phone, and I wanted to learn all about the person who made this piece of technology possible. Plus, I get to do some of my research on my phone, which means my parents can't get mad at me for being on . . . 'a device.'"

Everyone laughs at Justin's jokes, but it quickly becomes obvious that while he's entertaining, he hasn't done a whole lot of actual research yet.

"More specifics about his life and work, Justin," Mr. Griffiths explains. "Remember, you will eventually need to be prepared well enough to not only speak as if you are Alexander Graham Bell, but to be able to answer questions about him too."

As Justin heads back to his seat, slapping hands with one of his friends on the way, Mr. Griffiths takes a moment to talk about appropriate online research and warns us that relying on Wikipedia will earn us a failing grade.

I raise my hand halfway the third time around, and this time Mr. Griffiths calls on me.

Here we go.

I take a deep breath, ignoring the trembling in my legs, and walk to the front of the class. Fighting the desire to run away, I search for a friendly face to focus on, clear my throat, and start to speak.

"Malala Yousafzai fights for education. She's from Pakistan, which is where my family is originally from. Malala loved going to school and wanted to be a doctor one day."

My hands are shaking slightly, but I hope no one can tell.

"After a while Malala was told that she and other girls couldn't go to school anymore by a group of people who were part of the Taliban. They came into her village and started changing the rules and doing things like forcing women to stay inside and banning movies."

Mr. Griffiths is taking notes, which I hope means something positive. Half the class appears to be listening to me, but a few are doodling or staring out the window, and one kid's eyes are closed. I think he might be asleep.

"Malala didn't want to stop learning, and she spoke up about her right to get an education. She kept going to school after she was threatened, and her father supported her. When she was fifteen, Malala was shot in the head by the Taliban while she was riding the school bus."

As I say the last line, the energy in the room changes. Suddenly everyone is paying attention. My nerves threaten to return, but Mr. Griffiths nods his head when I glance at him, as if to say, "Go on." I exhale and try to remember to speak slowly.

"She had to be flown to England and have a bunch of operations, but she miraculously survived and recovered," I continue.

"And even though she was almost killed, she refused to stop speaking up for the rights of all girls to be educated. She won a Nobel Peace Prize when she was only sixteen, and she's the youngest person to ever get that honor. Malala's working on a bunch of programs to help girls and fight for their right to an education, and she travels around the world inspiring people with her story and her bravery."

I rush through the end and start to return to my seat, until Mr. Griffiths holds up a hand to stop me.

"Just a moment." Mr. Griffiths clears his throat. "What sources are you using, Amina?"

"A few books I checked out and some articles."

"Have you read her autobiography *I Am Malala*?" Mr. Griffiths asks.

"No."

"If we don't have it at our library, I'm certain it's at the Greendale Public Library. It's always helpful to have firsthand accounts if possible. Remember, class, getting information from a variety of reliable sources, primary, secondary, helps us to get the full picture. But, nice job."

As I head back to my seat, my insides start to unwind. I managed to get through speaking for two whole minutes in front of an audience, which I think is the longest ever. And Mr. Griffiths thinks I'm doing okay so far.

"Oh my gosh. That is *so* awful, what happened to Malala," a girl named Sheila says to me as I sit back down. "I can't believe anyone could do something like that."

"Yeah, I know." I nod in agreement.

"It makes me so sad that all those girls in Pakistan don't have rights like we do," Sheila adds, pushing out her lower lip for emphasis, and I stop nodding.

Wait. What?

"Yeah, we're so lucky we don't live there," the girl sitting next to her declares, and then Sheila adds, "Can you imagine?" with a dramatic sigh. A few others murmur their agreement.

Shame creeps up from the back of my neck into my face as Sheila's eyes bore into me, as she waits for me to say something. It's as if she expects me to comfort her, or maybe she wants me to agree with her. But no words find their way to my tongue, which is frozen like I feared it would be earlier. And any confidence I had when I walked back to my seat oozes out of me.

I desperately search for Mr. Griffiths, with the hope that he'll jump in and say what I'm unable to. Something like "Girls in Pakistan do have rights—it's the Taliban that tried to take them away." Or maybe that there are millions of other girls in Pakistan whose experiences aren't anything like Malala's. Girls like Zohra and my other cousins, who are safe and comfortable and living perfectly ordinary lives.

But Mr. Griffiths is talking to a kid on the other side of

the room and looking at something in his binder, and he didn't hear her.

What am I supposed to say?

Before I say anything, Mr. Griffiths asks who wants to go next, and Sheila waves her hand around and then pops out of her seat. She doesn't look sad anymore as she walks to the front of the room and, with a toss of her hair, delivers an energetic presentation about Amelia Earhart.

"Amelia Earhart taught us that, for men and women alike, the sky is the limit!" She squeals like a cheerleader at the end. She beams, and then, after glancing in my direction, adds dramatically, "At least in America."

My heart sinks and is a rock sitting in my stomach for the rest of the day.

20

"What exactly did she say, geeta?" Baba pulls his chair up closer to the table and puts his napkin in his lap.

"That she was sad girls in Pakistan don't have rights. And then another girl said we're lucky we don't live there."

"Ouch!" Mustafa shakes his head.

"I know. It was so—" I drop my head and don't finish my thought.

"Ignorant?" Mustafa volunteers.

"No. I mean, well, yeah, but it was so . . . *embarrassing*." I half whisper the last word.

Mama hears me and clucks her tongue. "What do you have to be embarrassed about?"

"That they think Pakistan is this horrible place."

Thaya Jaan's words come rushing back to me, from the day I said good-bye to him. He asked me to show people the beauty of Pakistan. Somehow I've managed to do the opposite. Now, because of me, everyone in History 7A thinks Pakistan is where girls get shot for trying to go to school.

Baba tears off a piece of naan that he uses to scoop up some daal.

"Listen," Baba says between mouthfuls. "The truth is, that did happen to Malala. And the people who did that—"

Baba wipes his mouth and clears his throat. When he continues to speak, his voice is deep and gravelly.

"The idea that anyone could harm an innocent girl for wanting to go to school is sickening. The people doing these things are illiterate fools themselves, led by some of the most corrupt humans on the planet. They are a disgrace to Muslims everywhere."

Mama nods her head. "Baba's right. And Malala's case got a lot of international attention, but sadly, poor girls suffer from injustice everywhere in the world. Including in America."

"People don't think of that," Mustafa says as he loads more meat on his plate.

"What people?" Baba asks.

"Take some salad, too," Mama insists, pushing the bowl closer to him. Mustafa picks out a few cucumbers and then hands me the salad. I take some of the lettuce and add it to my plate.

"People like the kids in Amina's class," Mustafa explains. "They don't think about other injustices. They hear about Malala and assume that's what all of Pakistan is like. That it's filled with poor people in villages, and terrorists who are going around shooting them."

"I doubt that," Mama says, but she doesn't sound convinced herself.

"You can't help it if that's literally the only thing you hear about a place," Mustafa continues. "Look at you, Amina. Even you were scared to go to Pakistan, because you didn't remember what it was really like and only heard about the crappy things that happen there, right?"

"Kind of," I say, although he's right. I had been scared, and I admitted it to Zohra that night on the roof.

"You were. You know it. And it's the same thing over there. Do you know Ahmed was actually asking me before we left to come home if it's safe for me to go to high school in America? They hear about school shootings here and think it happens every day."

The rock inside my gut is back, and it flips over. I don't want to think about anyone getting shot, anywhere. I wonder if it's too late for me to switch the subject of my project, to be someone, anyone, other than Malala. But we're already halfway through the quarter, I've done so much work on her, and our big performance is less than a month away.

"Let's talk about something nice," Mama pleads. "This isn't pleasant dinner conversation."

"It's life, jaani," Baba says to Mama. "The kids have to face these things."

"It's garbage." Mustafa shakes his head.

"Well, that's why we have to do our part to learn the truth and to educate others," Mama says.

"That sounds like something my teachers say," Mustafa snorts.

"Well then, see? I'm smart like your teachers." Mama smiles thinly.

"Yeah, except for no one says how we're supposed to do that."

Mama shrugs. "I wish I knew."

I wish I knew too. I need to know.

Everyone eats in silence for a few minutes and tries to digest these heavy thoughts. I nibble on my naan and think about what Mustafa said. What if I focus on the other parts of Malala's life that I learned about, more than the shooting? My class has already heard about that, so maybe when I dress up as Malala, I can talk about everything else she's been doing.

"How's the team?" Mama asks Mustafa. "Are the new kids having fun playing basketball?"

"They're trying." Mustafa grimaces. "Some of them don't

have a way to get to the Islamic Center if their parents don't drive or have cars."

"Maybe we can form a car pool or get them rides," Mama offers.

"A few don't understand basketball. Or never played before," Mustafa adds. "We're going to get destroyed. Even worse than last season."

"I'm sure you'll figure it out," Mama reassures him. "And I've been meaning to tell you there's another apartment setup happening this weekend. Salma Auntie and I thought you kids could help."

"Sure," Mustafa and I both say. I welcome something to get my mind off of everything, from Malala to worrying about Thaya Jaan. That reminds me that I haven't heard anything about his doctor appointment today.

"How's Thaya Jaan doing?" I ask.

My parents look at each other, and Baba lets out a little sigh.

"It looks like he might need surgery, but we're getting a second opinion," he says.

Mustafa puts down his fork and hangs his head. I feel something tug in my chest when I hear the word "surgery."

Mama coughs and sips her water. "Just keep praying for whatever is best for him, okay?"

I nod and take a bite of my keema, remembering the time my uncle told me that the spicy minced meat was his favorite dish when he was a kid. He listed all the different things his mother would put in it, like cauliflower, peas, onions, and his least favorite, turnips that masqueraded as the much more palatable potato until he bit into them.

And now I'm sitting on the other side of the world, failing him as I eat food that comes from the country I'm suddenly confused about. It's like delicious keema ruined by something bitter like turnips. How can something be so wonderful and yet so disappointing at the same time?

21

Mama is out of breath when she gets to the top of the stairs, and I'm panting a bit myself.

"I need to do more cardio," Mama groans. "This is bad."

We had to climb three sets of stairs to get to the apartment we're setting up and are each carrying an armload of bedding. I want to wipe the sweat off my forehead but don't know where to put the bags down.

"Leave that stuff with me." Mama motions to the space outside the door, and I drop the comforters and blankets in a heap and mop my brow with my sleeve. "Can you and Mustafa grab the rest of the things from the trunk while I set up the kitchen? I'm not doing those stairs again."

I don't point out to Mama that the stairs would provide the cardio workout she was just talking about and search for Mustafa instead. He's helping to assemble a bunk bed in one of the bedrooms. A man with a toolbox is directing Yusuf, who's bolting together two pieces that Mustafa is holding. I find Rabiya in one of the other bedrooms arranging toys on a bookshelf.

"I have to get the rest of the things from the car. Can you come?" I ask.

"Okay." Rabiya props up a Little Mermaid figurine next to a lamp shaped like a shell. "We tried to make this room underwater themed. Like Atlantis."

"Cute."

"My mom said that there are four kids, and the three boys are going to share the other room, but the girl gets her own. I wish we could paint it turquoise."

"How old are they?"

"I don't know."

There's a random assortment of toys that have clearly been played with before they made it to this apartment. I wonder what kinds of things the kids moving here will like, and what they had to leave behind. Will this little girl know who Ariel is? Or about My Little Pony? Or do they have different characters in Afghanistan?

A bunch of people came to help today, and we needed all of them to unload a U-Haul truck filled with sofas, a small dining table and chairs, pieces of beds, and a pile of mattresses. When we walked into the empty apartment, which had nothing in it but dim ceiling lights and worn beige carpets, I didn't believe that we'd be done by noon. But two hours later, only the beds and kitchen are left to set up.

As Rabiya and I climb back down the three flights of stairs, I try not to notice the stains on the steps or the musty odor that smells faintly of overripe fruit. We manage to bring all of the things left in the trunk in one trip: throw pillows, a few framed prints for decorations, and a jumbo bag of rice and some spices from the Indian market that Mama and I picked up yesterday.

"I wish they had a real sofa set," Rabiya says as we lug the bags up the stairs.

"Isn't that a real sofa set?" I ask.

"They had to split a sectional into two parts to make it fit in the room. You can see where it's supposed to be connected."

We enter the apartment, and Rabiya points to the sides of the sofa, which are an ugly shade of beige instead of the navy blue velvet fabric that covers the rest of it.

"See? Right there. It's like it's broken." The edges of Rabiya's mouth droop, and her eyes start to fill up. As I watch her struggle with her emotions, I understand why. Rabiya wants everything to be nice for this family, or at least closer to what she has. That's how I feel too. My chest tightens as I imagine what it would be like to walk into a strange new place, filled with other people's old toys and extra bedding, and have to call it home.

What if your heart still lives somewhere else?

"We can cover it with this blanket, and some of these pillows," I suggest.

When we're done draping the soft tan blanket over the edge of the sofa, you can hardly see the parts that don't match. And the bright orange pillows are cheerful. Rabiya steps back, checks it out, and nods, satisfied. As a finishing touch, she props up one of the framed prints, some Arabic calligraphy, on the side table.

"Much better." She nods as I arrange a few books on the coffee table to hide the scratches.

We take the rice and spices into the kitchen, where Mama and Salma Auntie are stacking storage containers in the cabinets.

"All set?" Mama asks when she sees me.

"Yeah." I nod.

Yusuf and Mustafa come out of the bedroom and ask us to check out the bunk bed they've finished. It's got stickers on it that are half peeled off, but it's cute, with a set of matching car bedspreads on it. On the floor is a smaller bed, with tiny wheels on it like you'd find on a suitcase.

"It looks great," Mama says.

"Who's the family that's living here?" I ask Mama.

"We don't know anything about them other than they're from Afghanistan and that there's a mother, father, and four kids."

"Do you know why they had to leave?"

"Only that the dad was working for different international organizations, and he started to get threats and his brother was kidnapped."

I think about Malala and wonder if the Taliban was behind the threats again, and a flash of anger bubbles inside me.

"Are we going to meet them?" Rabiya asks.

"I hope so," Mama says. "A church group is going to welcome them at the airport and bring them dinner tonight."

"Can we eat now?" Yusuf asks at the mention of dinner.

"Yes. Let's get some lunch," Mama says. "You've been working hard."

"Can I ride with you and Amina?" Rabiya asks.

"Sure," Mama says. "But where should we go?"

"How about Afghani food?" Mustafa asks. "Isn't there a place around here? Can I drive?"

"The owner of the Afghan restaurant near here donates meals to welcome new families. Let's go there," Salma Auntie agrees.

"No driving today," Mama says to Mustafa. "Not with Amina and Rabiya in the car."

Mustafa starts to protest but quits when he sees that Mama isn't going to budge. Rabiya and I turn around and examine the apartment one last time while Mustafa snaps a few photos of it. It's completely different from where we live, but it actually feels inviting now. And like Baba said, it's a safe place and a fresh start for people who can't be in their own homes anymore. I try to focus on that, instead of why they had to leave, as Rabiya grabs my hand and we head out.

22

"Why won't you show me?" Rabiya whispers.

"I can't believe you looked at it!" I snap.

"I didn't know what it was," Rabiya insists. "I thought maybe it was something else for the apartment. But then I saw your handwriting."

"It says 'PRIVATE' in plain English on the cover," I grumble.

"I didn't see that. It was upside down!"

"What are you two whispering about?" Mama asks.

"Nothing," I say quickly. Rabiya noticed the notebook I had left in the backseat of the car when we went to get the rest of the items for the apartment. And of course she peeked inside while we drove to lunch, without asking my permission, and read the lyrics and notes I've been scribbling down. Now she wants to talk about it. But the last thing I want is for everyone else to know about it and to have opinions.

"Can we have a sleepover?" Rabiya takes the opportunity to ask what was going to come up eventually anyway.

Mama turns to Salma Auntie, who shrugs.

"Up to you," she says. "Do you want my kids on your hands?"

"It's okay with me. But you two know the deal," Mama warns.

"We know, we know. No complaining about Sunday school in the morning," Rabiya says.

"Want to come?" Mustafa asks Yusuf, as if there's a possibility he doesn't want to hang out and play video games all night. Yusuf nods since his mouth is full. I take another bite of this place's famous rice. It's buttery with carrots and raisins cooked in it. Rabiya thinks cooked carrots are disgusting and picked them all out, but I love the way the slightly sweet rice mixes with salty ground beef kabobs and chunks of juicy chicken. I hope we can come back to this restaurant another time with Baba, since he had to make rounds at the hospital today and couldn't join us.

"Anyone want this?" Mama holds out a plate with a ravioli-like dish with meat inside and, when everyone refuses, scrapes the last of it onto her own plate. "Alhamdulillah. This was an amazing meal," she says.

"Yeah," we all agree.

"Do you have room for dessert?" Salma Auntie asks. "I saw rice pudding on the menu."

"No thank you," I say. "I'm stuffed."

"I hope they get the new family dinner from here tonight," Rabiya adds.

"Maybe they should welcome them with pizza or something American," Yusuf suggests.

When Thaya Jaan came to visit last year, we didn't understand why Mama went overboard cooking elaborate Pakistani feasts for him, including the dishes usually reserved for dinner parties. We were certain he'd prefer things like fried chicken and burgers. But she was right—our uncle didn't like to eat out at first, until Mustafa gradually got him to come around. By the time he left, we could count on him to agree to get our favorites with us.

"I think something familiar might be comforting to them," Salma Auntie says. "They'll have plenty of time to eat pizza. Don't you kids ever get tired of it?"

"Never." Yusuf shakes his head.

"Not in a million years," Mustafa adds.

"Let's get some tonight," Yusuf says.

"I'm in." Mustafa and Yusuf grin at each other while Mama and Salma Auntie roll their eyes in disbelief.

"Remember when I used to follow Yusuf around with bites of food while he played with his toys to get him to eat?" Salma Auntie laughs. "Now he won't stop eating!"

Mustafa and Yusuf grin wider and slap hands. I can't help but agree with the moms when they complain about how a new box of cereal only lasts two days. I'm lucky if I get more than a single bowl out of a box if it's the kind Mustafa likes.

• • •

When we get home, I run ahead of Rabiya into my room and tuck my notebook into a drawer so it's out of sight, hoping she'll forget about it. But we're barely hanging out for five minutes before she starts to interrogate me.

"So, what is it? Poetry? Is it for school? Or like a diary?" Rabiya is sprawled over the carpet on my floor, leaning on a giant teddy bear that's permanently squashed from being used as a pillow for years.

"It's nothing." I try to keep my face blank.

"Come on, Amina. Why are you keeping secrets from me?" Rabiya's face clouds, and she picks at the little bit of fluff that's coming out of poor Teddy's leg.

"It's not secrets. I'm writing about things I've been thinking about."

Rabiya pauses and plays with the fluff in her hand.

"So, are you, like, having an identity crisis?" she asks after a moment.

"A what?" I sit up straight so I can see her face properly. "Are you kidding?"

Rabiya props herself up on an elbow and meets my gaze. Her expression is serious.

"I mean, I don't know. My mom was saying my cousin who's a little older than you is having one."

"So?"

"Well the stuff you wrote was all 'who am I' and 'where do I fit in' and—"

"You weren't supposed to read that, remember?"

"It was an accident!" Rabiya insists.

"You accidentally opened up my notebook and then you accidentally read my private thoughts?"

"I told you already I didn't realize what it was. And I didn't read that much."

I stare at her in disbelief.

"But anyway," Rabiya continues, looking down. "You seem to be a bit—I don't know—out of it lately. Are you okay?"

"I'm fine," I mumble, although I'm not convinced of that myself.

Am I having an identity crisis?

"What's going on with you?" Rabiya's eyes narrow.

"You've been different since you came back from Pakistan."

"Different how?"

"Like, all serious and sad."

"No I'm not!"

"You are." Rabiya nods her head slowly in her "trust me, I know" kind of way.

I flop back on my bed and stare at the stick-on stars on my ceiling. They used to make me happy when they glowed at night, but right now they're fake and annoying.

I blink hard, as my friend's words sting, and wonder what's going on in my head. The truth is I have been unsettled since we came home, and nothing is right. I miss everything about Pakistan so much but have begun to wonder if I belong there at all now that I'm back. I'm happy to be home and to see everyone, but they either don't understand what I'm feeling or act like they don't care. On top of all that, thinking about the Malala project and worrying about Thaya Jaan has my head spinning.

The only thing that has helped is pouring out my thoughts into that notebook—a string of words trying to make sense of what's going on inside me. But now that Rabiya is asking about it, it seems silly and pointless. I don't want to share it and have her think it's weird, or too emotional, or that I've changed for the worse.

"I miss Pakistan," I finally say. "And everyone over there. So much. Especially Zohra."

"Well, you're here now," Rabiya mutters.

"Yeah. I'm aware," I reply.

"In case you didn't notice, I'm still here too." Rabiya doesn't bother to mask the bitterness in her voice. She pulls a photo album off my shelf and starts to flip through it. It's a signal that the conversation is over.

I feel a pinch of guilt because I can tell she's hurt. Rabiya has always been there for me. No matter what else is going on with my family or my other friends, I've been able to count on her. But she doesn't get what's going through my head right now and doesn't want to hear about my connections to Pakistan, and especially to Zohra. And I don't know how to explain it all to her either. Right now, I need some space to figure myself out first.

23

The school dance committee tried hard to transform the cafeteria into something nicer. All of the tables are hidden away, except for the ones being used that are covered in red tablecloths. Bunches of balloons brighten the corners of the room. And a big banner screams WELCOME BACK, COUGARS.

A bearded DJ with a shaved head is set up in a corner with a laptop that has colorful stickers all over it and a set of jumbo speakers. He's wearing big headphones and a look of concentration as he presses buttons on the computer that send music blasting out into the room.

Ms. Holly is on the opposite side of the room holding a plastic cup and talking to a few other teachers. Mr. Griffiths isn't here, which doesn't surprise me. I imagine him sitting at home watching the History channel or reading a massive biography in front of a crackling fireplace.

"I love this song," Soojin shouts so I can hear her. She's wearing the baby-blue dress from the photo, and her hair is tied up in a messy bun. I try not to envy how the pastel straps contrast with her tanned shoulders and arms.

I'm in an orange maxi dress that reaches my ankles, with a cropped white cardigan. Mama forced me to put it on, since the dress is sleeveless. It would be a lot cuter without it, but I promised to wear it this way when Mama agreed to let me get the dress.

Like she predicted, Emily is wearing something a lot fancier than most people. It's satiny and puffy and looks like one of those bridesmaid's dresses people make fun of in movies. She tugs on it and frowns.

"I told you my mother would get me something that's too much!"

"You look great," Soojin says, soothing her. "And don't worry—it's dark in here!"

I choke back a laugh, which makes Emily grin, and she does a little curtsy.

"Come on, let's dance before I chicken out and hide in the bathroom," she says.

Soojin grabs my hand and tries to pull me into the center of the cafeteria, which has been taped off to form a dance floor. She moves gracefully, with the confidence of someone used to performing, which is completely unfair to everyone else in the room.

I, on the other hand, am the total opposite of Soojin. My feet are heavy as I trudge behind her, and while I hear the beat of the music, my body isn't interested in moving to it. I'd much rather sing along and remain stationary.

But no one else is singing, and my friends want to dance, so I shake my shoulders a bit and try to mimic the arm movement Emily is doing—a kind of pointing into the air—until I feel stupid. I stop midway and put my arm down, leaving it awkwardly dangling by my side, wondering how quickly I can say I'm thirsty and need to get a drink.

"It's hot in here," I finally yell to Soojin after another thirty seconds. "I'm going to get some water."

Soojin points to my cardigan.

"Take that off," she says.

"I'm okay." I shake my head. "I'm going to get a drink."

"Come back quick," Soojin says, and I know she's figured out that I'm trying to escape.

"I will," I promise.

I squeeze past people and make my way over to the drink table, which is loaded with jugs of water and lemonade. Our principal, Mr. Little, is serving students.

"Lemonade, please," I say, but as I start to sip it, I get more overheated. I decide to duck into the empty hallway where no one will see me to cool off for a couple of minutes.

"Going home?" a voice asks as I step into the science wing, making me jump and almost spill my drink.

I look around and find Nico, sitting on the floor in front of the lockers with his legs sticking out in front of him.

"You scared me!" I say. "What are you doing out here?"

"Hiding," he says.

"From what?"

"All of it. I'm not much of a party person. And I can enjoy the music better out here."

"Why'd you come at all, then?"

"Mom forced me. She said it'd be good for making friends." Nico shrugs.

"Right." I smile.

"What about you?" Nico asks. "Who are you hiding from?"

"No one." I decide that's not totally a lie. "I was hot."

"Gotcha. Do you think we should dance?" Nico stands up and loosens the striped blue tie he's wearing over a gray shirt.

"I don't want to go back in there." I hesitate.

Nico peers back into the cafeteria. "Yeah, it's kind of scary," he agrees.

"And I don't dance," I admit.

"I figured."

Blood rushes to my face.

Is he saying he thinks I'm a dork?

"I don't dance either." Nico smiles in a way that feels kind and pushes the hair out of his eyes. I exhale as he continues to speak.

"My cousin always said he didn't know how to dance, and then he suddenly learned before a family wedding," Nico says. "He busted out with all these fancy moves that he learned from watching YouTube."

"Was he any good?" I ask, trying to imagine it.

"He was okay, but you could see in his face that he was trying to remember the steps."

Nico imitates his cousin's moves and looks so ridiculous when he does a little spin that I burst out laughing.

"Your turn." Nico points to me, and I surprise myself by playing along.

"I haven't been to a wedding in a while. But when I was in Pakistan, we were dancing around one day to be silly, and my cousin showed us something like this."

I demonstrate one of the bhangra moves Ahmed tried to teach Mustafa and me, with little success. It involves jumping with your legs sticking out sideways and shaking your shoulders with your arms and hands up. Nico copies what I'm doing and is better than me.

"That's like Bollywood, right?" Nico asks.

"Yeah." I stop, confused. "How do *you* know about Bollywood?"

"My family's Egyptian. Everyone in Egypt loves Bollywood movies. They're on TV all the time."

"You're Egyptian?"

"Half. My mother's side. My father's French."

"Oh." I examine Nico more closely, as if he's suddenly going to seem different to me. He stares back until I look away.

"My sister is obsessed with Shah Rukh Khan movies," Nico adds. "I had to watch him in *Dilwale* three times."

"You should check out *Amar Akbar Anthony*. It's old, but funny," I suggest.

"Maybe."

Soojin pokes her head outside the cafeteria doors, and her eyes grow wide when she sees me and Nico together. Then she disappears back into the cafeteria.

I totally forgot I said I would be quick.

"My friends are looking for me," I say, suddenly warm again. "I better find them."

"Yeah, me too."

"You're going to find my friends?"

"No, I meant mine." Nico grins. "I do have a few."

"Right, I know," I say as my cheeks flush. "See you in class."

"Bye, Amina." Nico and I head in opposite directions as we enter the cafeteria. I know I'm going to hear it from Soojin and Emily. But I'm glad my friends convinced me to come tonight, and I walk back toward the dance floor with lighter feet than before.

24

"Can I talk to Thaya Jaan?" I've been sitting on the sofa listening to Baba ask him a thousand questions about his health for the last fifteen minutes. I want a turn to say hi and to see his face, especially since I've been thinking about him so much.

I know Baba is thinking about him too. The worry lines in his forehead seem deeper than before, and Mama says he needs to stop stressing so much or he'll make himself sick. The problem is my father's convinced that surgery is Thaya Jaan's best option.

"Is that my geeta?" I hear Thaya Jaan asking, so Baba hands over the tablet, and I say salaam.

"Walaikum assalaam warahmatullahi wabarakatuh,"

Thaya Jaan responds, giving me extra blessings. He's lying back on his chair and holding a cup of chai in his hands. His favorite topi is on his head, the one that's shaped like a mushroom but still manages to make him look cool.

"What are you doing?" I ask. I've already heard him answer all the questions about his health and want to talk to him about anything else.

"I was watching a cricket match when your dad called." Thaya Jaan smiles at me. "And thinking about how I wanted to talk to you. And now my wish came true."

"Me too." I smile back.

"How about you? How's school?"

"It's fine."

"How's your special project coming? Are you learning a lot about Malala?"

"Yeah," I mumble.

All I can think about is what the others in my class said after my research update. But I don't want to tell him about that. Thaya Jaan waits for me to elaborate, but I don't know what else to say.

"What are you thinking, geeta?" Thaya Jaan asks. He's still able to read me, even from thousands of miles away. "Is there something else?"

"No," I lie. "Are you feeling okay?"

Just like that, I ask Thaya Jaan about his health, after I was trying to avoid it.

"I'm doing okay." Thaya Jaan coughs slightly.

"Soojin's dad told me he hopes you get better soon." Mr. Park was at school to pick up Soojin this afternoon, and he asked about Thaya Jaan. Soojin must have told him that he's been having health issues.

"How's their restaurant going? I enjoyed that delicious beef dish."

"Fine, I think." That reminds me that we haven't been to the Park Avenue Deli in a while, and next time it's my turn to choose where to eat out, I'm going to pick it.

"We need a Korean place in Lahore," Thaya Jaan says. "Maybe they can expand here someday."

"That would be awesome. How's Thayee?"

"She's doing well. Visiting her sister right now. But I

think I'm worrying her quite a bit. Along with the rest of you."

"We're okay." I say that so Thaya Jaan won't feel guilty, but then I hope he doesn't think I mean that we aren't thinking about him.

"I tell her jo hona hai, hoga," Thaya Jaan says. "It's in Allah's hands."

Despite my poor Urdu, I understand him. It means something like "what will be, will be."

"Yeah." I gulp. "But you'll get better soon."

You have to.

"Should I call Zohra?" Thaya Jaan asks. "She's upstairs."

He starts to lift himself out of his chair, but it seems to be taking so much effort that I stop him.

"It's okay, Thaya Jaan. I have to go to the grocery store with Mama."

"Okay, geeta." Thaya Jaan puts a hand over his heart. "Khuda hafiz."

"Khuda hafiz."

"And, Amina," Thaya Jaan adds before signing off. "I'm

proud of you for sharing Malala's story with your classmates."

I gulp again, swallowing my guilt, when I think about the things the kids in my class were saying about Malala's story. But I nod to Thaya Jaan and vow to do better. I want to keep my promise to him. I owe it to everyone who loves Pakistan—to him, my parents, Zohra, even Malala. And I owe it to myself.

25

"Did you quit drama club?" Nico asks me after the bell rings, and we file out of chorus at the end of the day.

"No. Why?"

"Because you weren't there yesterday?"

"Oh. Right. I had to help my mom with . . . something."

Nico laughs. "That sounds like the fakest excuse ever."

The truth is I was disappointed when Mama texted and said she had to pick me up right after school. She needed me to go with her and Mustafa to get a bunch of kitchen stuff from this older auntie who lives in Bayside.

"No, for real," I insist. "My mom sets up apartments for refugees. And she got a call from someone who was moving and wanted to donate a bunch of dishes and decorations. It was all nice, so she made me skip so we could collect it."

"Gotcha. I was just messing with you."

"Oh." I can't tell when Nico is teasing since his expression doesn't change at all. It doesn't help with his hair covering half of his face like usual.

"But that's cool about the apartments. Can other people sign up to help?" he asks.

"Like who?"

"Like me."

"Really? Um. I don't know. I guess so." I try to picture Nico in the apartment with us, building beds with Mustafa and Yusuf or setting up sofas with Rabiya and me.

"My mom's been getting on me to do some volunteering," Nico explains. "And I'm pretty good at carrying stuff."

"It's fun. You go in and turn an empty apartment into a home."

"Nice." Nico waits for me to say something else. But I'm not sure what it is.

"What?"

"So, you'll ask?" he says, and as he pushes back his hair, his eyes are earnest.

"I'll ask," I promise.

"Will you be there next week?" Nico asks. "At drama club?"

"I think so."

"You can't leave me there all alone," Nico says.

I give him a wave and start to turn the corner since I have to get my lunch bag from my locker.

"Hey. Do you want to come over?" Nico calls after me. "We can make beats."

I stop walking.

Is he serious?

"Right now? I don't know if I—" I turn back as a familiar warmth fills my face.

"That's all right," Nico quickly interjects. "I thought you wanted to learn."

"I do! But . . . maybe you could come to my house instead?" The words tumble out of my mouth before I've had the chance to think them through.

"That works." The parts of Nico's face I can see are smiling. "I'll meet you at the bus line."

Nico walks away, and I start to sweat. I have no idea what my mom will think about me inviting over a boy she doesn't know. But there's a better chance of her being okay with that than with me going to his house. I whip out my phone and type a message to her.

Hi Mama. Can a friend

I delete the word "friend."

Can this boy

I delete the entire message and start over.

Is it okay if this kid comes over to work on a project after school?

Then I change "kid" to "guy." But that sounds worse.

Can someone from my class come over to work on a project today?

I hit send.

By the time I get to my locker, Mama has written back.

Sure.

I wonder if I should mention it's a boy, because I don't

want her to be surprised when she gets home. But how do I say that now, without making it a big deal? I decide to say nothing.

Soojin has a hard time containing her shock when Nico walks up to us while we're standing in the bus line.

"You're on the Orange bus, right? Will your driver care if I don't have a note?" he asks.

"No, Freddie doesn't mind as long as we aren't loud," I say, watching as Soojin's jaw literally drops open. She starts to squeeze my arm, and I know exactly what she's thinking.

"Do you have your laptop?" I ask Nico as I brush Soojin's hand off my arm and try to show her that it's all business.

"Right here." Nico pats his backpack.

"Doesn't it get heavy?"

"Nah. I work on stuff at lunch sometimes and after school, so I want to have it with me."

"What are you guys doing?" Soojin asks. Her eyes are dancing, and I can tell she wants to say more.

"I'm showing Amina how to make beats," Nico says.

"Interesting." Soojin gives me a sideways look, like she doesn't quite believe him.

"You want to come?" Nico offers.

"Oh, uh, no, I can't." Soojin's brow furrows, and she backs away from the unexpected invitation. "I have to go to dance now. Have fun." Before she turns around to walk to her bus, she gives me a signal that I know means "Call me after and tell me everything . . . or else!"

I file onto the bus behind Nico, suddenly remembering my old friend Mario from back in kindergarten, or maybe even preschool. We were inseparable, and Mama and Mario's mom used to arrange playdates at the park for us on the weekends. I have a strong memory of when they came over once and we made giant cookies with M&M's in them.

When Mario's family moved to Chicago, we managed to see them every now and then before eventually stopping. I haven't thought about Mario in years and wonder what happened to him. One thing was different back then: No one thought it mattered that Mario was a boy and my best friend or made it awkward.

I slide into the seat next to Nico, and my palms start to sweat.

Is everyone else making it awkward, or is it me?

26

The bus ride home flies by. Nico and I chat about our favorite music, and he talks about how different Greendale is from his old neighborhood in Madison. I learn that Nico's family moved here over the summer because of his mom's job. Instead of visiting Cairo like usual, they had to spend the summer packing up the house he'd lived in his whole life.

It's fun to compare Cairo to Lahore and realize how so many things are similar. Especially the traffic. Nico asks me about my family in Pakistan, what I did during our visit, and what it's like there. I believe him when, after I answer all of his questions and we arrive at my bus stop, he announces, "I want to go there someday."

. . .

"Should I take off my shoes?" Nico asks as we walk into the house.

"Yes, please."

Nico slips off his sneakers and lines them up neatly on the mat by the door. "This is nice," he says as he looks around.

"Thanks." I notice Nico surveying the padded bench by the shoe rack and the tiny framed mirrors in the entryway.

"Hey." Mustafa is sprawled in his usual spot on the sofa watching an episode of the latest show he's bingeing and doesn't look up when we come into the room.

"Hi," Nico responds.

Mustafa sits straight up and hits pause.

"Does Ma know you have a . . . um . . . friend over?" His eyes are bulging out of his face.

"Yeah, I texted her."

"Okay." Mustafa leans back again but doesn't hit play, and I can feel his stare as I lead Nico away into the kitchen.

"Are you hungry?" I ask as Nico goes straight to the sink

and washes his hands. Baba would appreciate that, and like he's reading my mind, Nico explains, "My mom's trained me. It's always the first thing I do when I get home."

"My dad's the same way," I laugh.

I pull out some chips and green grapes and pour us some juice. We sit at the table with our freshly washed hands, and Nico takes off his backpack and slides out his laptop.

When he rests the computer on the table, I make sure to push our glasses far away from it. Last year, Mustafa spilled milk, and the tiniest bit got into Mama's laptop and ruined it. When the technicians opened it up, they found cheese curds inside.

"Check this out." Nico opens the workstation on his computer, and all the boxes light up the screen. He hits play, and a thumping bass with some piano melodies on top fills the room.

"What is it?" I ask.

"Something new I'm working on."

"I like it," I say. "Even more than the last song you did."

"Thanks. I'm playing around with new sounds." Nico

helps himself to some chips and then wipes the crumbs off on his jeans.

"Can you show me from the beginning how you make a song? Like, all of the steps?" I ask.

"Sure."

Nico loads up an old-school soul sample, which means he was paying attention on the bus when I said what I listen to.

"First I use this scissor tool right here to chop up the sample like this," he says. His eyes are intense as he concentrates on what he's doing, and he bites his lower lip.

Next we listen to each snippet and choose our favorites, which Nico splices together. The trick, Nico shares, is to do it in a way that fits with the tempo he set.

"That's so awesome." I'm sitting on the edge of my seat the whole time Nico works and realize I'm hardly breathing. I force myself to sit back, take few deep breaths, and sip my juice.

"And now . . ." Nico watches me for a second before he starts to tap keys. "We need to add some drums."

Nico explains that the keys are programmed to the

sampler of a drum kit he loaded earlier. I listen as each tap adds another element, like a clap or snare.

When Nico plays what we have so far, I hear something that's starting to come together but is not nearly a song yet. It's a bit rough and repetitive.

"How do you get it from this to, like, an actual, real song?" I ask.

"We need to add some bass, and then we can mix and master it." Nico says "we," but he's the one doing everything while I'm writing down the steps in my notebook.

Nico opens up a bass synthesizer and uses the computer keys to lay down a bass line. It's deep and thumping, and our heads start to bob to the beat automatically.

Right then Mama walks into the kitchen from the garage.

"Hello," she says as she sees us. One eyebrow goes up, but she puts on a polite smile and comes forward as Nico hits pause and quickly stands to greet her.

"I'm Amina's mom," she says, looking back and forth at me and Nico. "And you are?"

"Nico Bertrand. Pleasure to meet you." Nico extends

his hand to Mama, who takes it and smiles more genuinely now. I can tell she's charmed. Mama always rates kids' manners and comments on who has the best ones.

"It's nice to meet you, too, Nico." Mama stares at me directly now. "What are you two working on, Amina? A project for what now?"

"Oh, um, Nico's in chorus and drama club with me. He's showing me how to put together a song on his digital audio workstation."

"It's called a DAW," Nico adds.

"I see." Mama looks puzzled, but she doesn't ask anything else. "Looks like you've had a snack. Can I get you anything else, Nico?"

"No thanks, Mrs. Khokar. I'm good."

Mama gives me a glance as she walks out of the kitchen, and I wish I could read her mind right now. And if I could, I'd remind her about Mario telepathically.

"We need to add a countermelody to accent the sample." Nico picks up where we left off as if nothing colossal just happened.

"What's that?"

"Like the finishing touch. Like how when—how do I explain it? Kind of like when chefs put those little leaves on top of fancy desserts."

"You mean garnish," Mustafa says as he comes into the kitchen. He leans over the back of the chair next to Nico.

Please don't say anything weird.

"Yeah, garnish. Thanks." Nico smiles.

There's a pause while we both wait to see what Mustafa wants.

"Amina, can you come in here for a minute?" Mama calls from the living room.

Mustafa gives me his "you're going to get it" look.

I ignore him, get up from my chair, and address Nico as calmly as I can, even though my insides are quaking.

"I'll be right back."

27

Mama is standing in the far corner of the room with her arms folded across her chest.

"I thought you were talking about inviting a girlfriend over," she says in a low voice. "Who is this boy?"

"Nico. He's new. And really nice."

Mama's eyebrow goes up again.

"And he's Egyptian," I add as an afterthought. "On his mom's side."

"Oh, so he's Muslim?" Mama seems instantly more relaxed.

"I don't know. But don't ask him, okay? That's so embarrassing," I plead.

"What's embarrassing about that? I have an Egyptian friend who might know his family."

"Mama!"

Mama shrugs. "It's a close-knit community, but fine. I can ask later. So . . . what are you working on?"

"Nico knows how to make music. Like how to produce songs. And he's showing me how."

"What for?"

"Because I want to learn how." I'm careful to keep my voice flat and not let the tiniest hint of sass escape my lips.

"So, this isn't schoolwork?"

"Not exactly. I'm learning for me."

Mama's frowning now, and it's like I can see the thoughts running through her mind.

"I told you, he's a nice guy. And he's smart. We're friends," I add.

"I don't know." Mama starts to shake her head. "What will your father think? You know we don't want you kids dating. Especially not in grade school."

"Eww! We're not dating," I whisper, grateful that the

music coming from the kitchen is loud enough that I can't make out what Mustafa is saying. Hopefully that means they can't hear us, either.

"He's like Mario." I continue to plead my case. "And a good person. He wants to help out with apartment setups."

"Mario? From kindergarten?" Mama's brow furrows.

"Yeah. Mario was my best friend, and he was a boy. Remember? It wasn't a problem back then. Girls and boys can be friends, can't they?"

"Well—I mean—yes—I suppose," Mama stammers.

"Well then it's okay, right?"

"I don't know, Amina. What about *his* intentions?"

"Mama! He just wants to be my friend." I pause and watch Mama fumble with the chain around her neck while she thinks before I add, "Can I go now?"

"Fine. We'll discuss this later." Mama squints, like she's trying to calculate a big number in her head.

"Okay." I give her a kiss, run back to the kitchen, and find Mustafa sitting in my chair with his face in the laptop.

"I like it," Mustafa is saying when he notices me standing

over him impatiently. "How do you add vocals?" he asks, slowly getting up and letting me take his place.

"With a better mic, but I don't have one," Nico says.

"Gotcha." Mustafa breaks off a bunch of the grapes sitting in the bowl and pops a few in his mouth. He turns to leave and then stops.

"You know Amina's got a voice, right?"

Mustafa is talking about me like I'm not sitting right here.

"That's what people say, but I haven't actually heard her sing yet."

"You should record her," Mustafa suggests.

"I want to." Nico turns to me, and I feel like I'm under a microscope and want to duck my head to avoid his gaze.

"Cool." Mustafa grabs a few more grapes and exits, and I'm glad we can get back to work.

"Your family's nice," Nico says once Mustafa is gone. "What's your brother's name?"

"Oh, shoot. It's Mustafa. Sorry I didn't introduce you."

"That's okay." Nico clears his throat. "I, uh, was already

going to ask you if you could maybe sing the hook for another song I'm working on. I just need to figure out how to record it."

"Yeah, sure. Maybe." That sounds so professional. Me . . . singing a hook! I try not to grin and act too eager.

"And maybe you can help me with lyrics?" Nico gives me a pleading look. "I stink at them."

"I'm not that great at them either," I admit. "I've been writing a bunch of stuff in this notebook, but it all feels wrong."

"You'll get there." Nico nods confidently, and I hope he's right.

"How about this?" I take a deep breath. "What if I help you with lyrics for your song and you help me with producing mine when it's ready?"

"Deal." Nico reaches his hand out. As I shake his, a tingle of electricity runs up my arm. But I tell myself it's from the thrill of producing original music and nothing else.

28

Malala's autobiography, *I Am Malala*, is better than the rest of the books I've read about her. It's as if the others took samples of her story and spliced them together. They spin a good story, but I'm glad to read her own words.

Malala describes her childhood village in the mountains of Swat so clearly I can imagine the crisp clean air, waterfalls, and jagged cliffs with narrow suspension bridges. The humble home she lived in sounds so different from Thaya Jaan's three-story house with its green gates, carport, manicured lawn filled with fruit trees and flowers, and my favorite veranda. However humble, though, Malala's village sounds like it was filled with happiness for many years, before the Taliban invaded.

I'm snuggled under a thick blanket on the couch and have been reading for so long that I don't notice it's getting dark outside until Baba switches on the lamp.

"Good book?" He sits down on the other end of the sofa and tickles my feet.

I pull my feet away and tuck them safely under me.

"Yeah, but it's so sad, Baba. I'm at the part where Malala talks about how the Taliban came into her village and ruined everything. They destroyed schools and blew up ancient treasures. They made men grow beards and forced women to cover up and stay inside. They threatened and killed people. . . ."

What would the kids in school think if they read this?

"I remember hearing about all that." Baba presses his lips together. "It was terrible."

Malala describes how the Taliban marred the walls of her father's school with threats because he allowed girls to attend. I couldn't help thinking of the awful words sprayed on our mosque last year and how much they frightened me. But in our case, the police came and investigated, everyone painted over the graffiti, and now the people behind it have been convicted of a crime. What if instead of that, someone simply told us they were changing the rules, and that we couldn't go there anymore, no matter what we wanted?

"I don't understand why people living there let the Taliban do everything they did," I admit. "Why didn't the police or the government stop them?"

"The Taliban came in and made gradual changes. When people finally woke up to what was happening and tried to stop them, the Taliban silenced them with threats and fear. Fear is the biggest factor."

"This whole time, I thought the Taliban was the enemy of America. But didn't the Afghani family we set up the apartment for have to escape and come here because of them?"

"They did." Baba shakes his head. "It's complicated."

"What if they take over the rest of Pakistan?" The question slips out of my mouth, and Baba acts surprised at first, and then moves closer and puts his arm around me.

"They won't, geeta."

"But they could, right? What if they do?"

"The government has control now. People are more aware, and they are rejecting these radical elements."

I want to believe Baba, but I'm still scared for my family that is there. I bite the side of my nail until Baba pulls my hand away. We sit together in silence, both thinking, until I speak again.

"Baba, are you proud to be from Pakistan?" Since we're talking about these things, I ask the question that I've been grappling with myself for days.

"Wow. That's a big question."

"Sorry."

"No, it's okay." Baba squeezes my shoulder. "You can ask me anything."

He reaches for his mug of tea from the side table and takes a sip.

"I am," Baba finally says. "Like we talked about the other day, every country has its challenges, including America. Every culture has shameful parts of its history and groups of people who do things that are wrong. Pakistan is no better or worse. But it's the land of my ancestors, filled with hard-working, smart, and kind people, and I am proud of it. Just as proud as I am to be American."

"If you weren't born there, would you be? Or if you were a girl?"

"You mean, if I was like you?"

I nod my head.

"I think I'd be feeling a lot like you."

I lean my head on Baba's chest and think about all the things that have been spinning through my brain ever since I talked to Zohra about her thinking she's unwelcome in America and shared my own fears about Pakistan. Back then, I thought about America as mine and Pakistan as hers. Now I think of them both as part of me, and I am proud of that, even if it is complicated.

"You know," Baba continues, "Pakistan has a lot of strong, independent, and brilliant women, in history, and today. Groups like the Taliban may be trying to hold them back. But the women will prevail. I know they will."

A wave of images and scenes from my trip to Pakistan

come crashing into my brain, but most of all, I think of Zohra. Images from my videos of her in action, pointing out sights from a rickshaw, telling me a story on the roof, and laughing so hard that we both gasped for air. I think of the day we sang together, and what she said about wanting to help her country.

I hope Baba is right. In her book, Malala describes the freedom, beauty, and respect for different beliefs in her village that were there before the Taliban, and hopefully will be there again. I witnessed so many wonderful things in Lahore when I was there this summer. And like Thaya Jaan asked of me, I can still try to help others see that there's so much beauty in a place that I love.

The doorbell rings and makes me jump.

"That must be Malik," Baba says.

I didn't know anyone was coming over, but when I throw open the door, Imam Malik is standing there with Sumaiya.

"Salaam!" I say, holding out my arms for Sumaiya, who nose-dives into my chest. She looks straight into my eyes and babbles a greeting.

"How are you, Amina?" Imam Malik asks as he pulls off Sumaiya's tiny pink sneakers and steps inside.

"I'm okay." Sumaiya wiggles out of my arms and starts to run into the house. "I got her."

"Thank you." Imam Malik wipes his forehead and follows us. "She's been up since fajr and moving nonstop."

"You can have a break. I'll play with her."

"You're the best." Imam Malik grins and quickly plops down on the sofa next to Baba, where I was sitting.

Sumaiya runs straight for the piano and tries to push the keyboard cover open. I'm not surprised she remembers it from the last time she was here. We played on it together for at least an hour.

I'm worried her little fingers will get crushed and scoop her into my arms, quickly sitting her on the bench next to me before she starts to wail. I open up the cover and let her bang on the black and white keys. And then I notice the sheet music for the Stevie Wonder song "Sir Duke" that's been sitting on the rack since before we left for our trip this summer and reread the lyrics in front of me. They talk about music being "a world within itself" and how it's "a language we all understand."

Sumaiya turns to me and giggles as she hits a high note. I give her a big kiss as a flash of inspiration pushes out the heavy thoughts in my head and fills me with unexpected hope.

29

Soojin's shirt matches the jade walls of her room. It's got tiny emojis all over it, and she's wearing pink-rimmed glasses, which make her seem younger than usual. But when she speaks to me, it's in a super-serious tone, like she's a lawyer on one of the crime dramas Mama watches.

"What did he say next?" she asks. "Tell us everything."

"That was it," I insist.

"Are you sure?" Emily swishes her ponytail back and forth. "He made a song for you, and he wants you to sing it? It sounds like he's super into you."

I sigh, while Emily grabs a handful of caramel popcorn from one of the bowls sitting on the sheet spread over Soojin's carpet.

"I'm not supposed to eat this stuff anymore," she confesses. "It's on the list."

Most of the snacks Soojin put out are foods Emily's orthodontist says she should avoid because of her new braces: chips, gummy candies, popcorn.

"It's like there's no point going to the movies again," Emily moans as she carefully chews each kernel. "You're so lucky your teeth are straight!"

"Do your braces hurt?" I ask, hoping that we can talk about teeth, homework, or anything other than Nico. Although I probably should have guessed I would be getting grilled about him. I texted my friends after he came over two days ago and told them everything that happened. But this is the first time the three of us have been alone together since then. And while Soojin said she wanted our help making a final round of campaign posters for her run for class president, I have a feeling getting together today might have had as much to do with Nico and me.

“They stopped hurting. But my mom will be so pissed if another bracket comes off.” Emily keeps eating the popcorn anyway.

“Can you hand me the Skittles?” I ask.

“So, like, don’t you think it’s strange that Nico is being so, I don’t know . . . friendly?” Emily hands me the box.

“We’re friends,” I repeat for the third time as I pick out my favorite red candies.

“I mean, you keep saying that,” Soojin pushes. “But the way it’s all so intense and you were hanging out at the dance alone and—”

“That wasn’t on purpose! I went into the hall, and he was there.”

Soojin cocks her head sideways like a pensive owl. “Okay, so tell us—what do you think is happening?”

“I don’t know,” I admit. “I like him. A lot. He’s nice, and he’s interested in my life, and he’s really into music, like me. But . . .” I pause, trying to think about how to express what I’m feeling. My friends seem so eager for me to *like* like him, but I honestly don't know if I do. "But it's not like I want him to be my boyfriend or anything." The words slip out of my mouth.

"Is it . . . because you're not allowed?" Soojin guesses.

"No, it's because I just don't." I try to stop questioning myself, or thinking about how to phrase things, and let myself talk.

"I mean, sometimes I get nervous around him, but I think that's because everyone else is watching us. Or maybe I'm excited to be friends with him. Or maybe . . ." I pause again, and the words jumble together in my head.

Soojin bites the head off a gummy bear and chews it slowly. Emily picks up a pen and clicks the top on and off. They both watch me, waiting for me to finish my thought.

"I don't know," I finally say, and my stomach starts to ache, possibly from the random assortment of things I've eaten in the last hour. "I told my mom we're just friends, and I meant it."

"I guess . . ." Soojin speaks as if she's thinking aloud. "You could just be excited to be friends."

"How do I know for sure?" I moan.

"You'll know when you know. You're young." Emily is solemn as she picks caramel out of her teeth.

"You sound like my mom." Soojin giggles, and throws a pillow at her.

"Stop! You're going to hurt my face!" Emily shields her mouth with her hands.

As I laugh with them, the churning inside me lessens. Maybe the fact that my friends are watching me closely as I interact with Nico doesn't mean they're pushing me to have a boyfriend. It could be that they're trying to protect me and making sure I'm okay. And maybe it's not the evil peer pressure my parents worry about after all.

"Can you and your new friend make me a campaign song?" Soojin asks. "I could ask the office to play it during the morning announcements."

"What kind of song?"

"I don't know. Something like 'Soojin Is Awesome,' to the tune of 'Everything Is Awesome'?"

"That would be ridiculous," Emily says. She arranges the

markers in rainbow order. "But we will make you some awesome signs."

"Fine," Soojin concedes. "But I still need something to set my campaign apart."

"What about making it about service?" I suggest.

"Like community service?"

"Yeah." I'm glad to change the subject and share what I've been mulling over since Imam Malik visited. I want to make Soojin's campaign stand out and be more than the same old tired promises and think I might have the answer.

"How?" Soojin leans closer to me and listens intently.

"I've been thinking about what I can do to make a difference lately. I help my mom with setting up apartments for refugee families sometimes, but I want to do more. Like my own project," I explain.

"Go on." Soojin grabs another handful of gummies and chews.

"My friend Rabiya wants me to make Eid cards and sell them to raise money, but you guys know my art skills suck."

"I mean, well, let's just say you're no Monet." Soojin

glances at the lettering on the poster I started and smiles.

"Right. So I thought about things I could do, that I'm good at. Like Mustafa coaching his basketball team."

"Singing?" Emily guesses.

"Yeah. Well, music. I thought I could teach kids who can't afford lessons how to play piano. Because music is something that brings everyone together, and it's a language everyone understands." I decide Stevie Wonder won't mind if I borrow from his song, especially since it gave me the idea to do this.

"How would you do it?" Soojin asks.

"I don't know yet. I need to figure that part out."

"I think that's great, Amina." Soojin doodles a heart and puts a bunch of smaller hearts inside it. "But what does it have to do with my campaign?"

"Everyone always says the same stuff. It's like 'Vote for me because I'm smart,' or 'I care about you,' or 'I'll fight for you.' But maybe you can be the person who cares about and wants to help people outside of school. And encourage other people to do that too."

"How?"

"I don't know—maybe you can say something like 'We can make a difference together' and start lists of ways to volunteer." I haven't figured out the details yet, but that sounds like a good start.

"Like on a poster?" Emily asks.

"Yeah, we can make the posters about this. And have sign-up sheets."

"Maybe if I do some service, I won't have to do chess club anymore." Emily brightens. "I'm so sick of playing chess. And my mom won't say no to me helping people."

"I think it's a great idea." Soojin nods thoughtfully. "I never liked the 'look at me' part of running for president."

Emily coughs extra hard and turns to me.

"Didn't you literally just ask me to make a 'Soojin Is Awesome' song?" I remind Soojin.

"I was KIDDING!" Soojin giggles again, and a pillow comes flying my way now.

I grab it and flop down on it, and we spend the next half hour working out the details of my idea. We also laugh and joke around and manage to finish the entire bowl of gummies without breaking off any of Emily's brackets.

As I watch my friends alternately tease me, ponder serious things, and stuff their faces with junk food, I conclude that they're still the best. Because even if my friends can't understand everything I've been going through lately, they're trying. And we can support one another while we do different things. As relief washes over me, I remember that I still need to make things right with someone else.

30

My body tenses when my phone starts to buzz, and I see that it's Zohra trying to FaceTime me early in the morning before Sunday school.

"Hello?" I get up from where I was sitting on the sofa and start to panic as Zohra's face appears. "Is everything okay?"

Zohra's teeth take up half the screen.

"Relax. Everything's fine. Abu is okay. I was missing you."

I exhale and dive back onto the couch, pulling the blanket over me, relieved it's nothing bad. My uncle finally has a surgery date scheduled for next week. Baba explained that doctors will open up his chest and create new arteries for blood to flow through, since some of his major ones are blocked. Thaya Jaan's been extremely lucky that his heart created new minor vessels around the blockages on its own, which prevented him from having a major heart attack. But now he needs a more permanent fix to get his blood pumping better.

Baba was calm and stuck to the science as he described it, although I know he's frightened about his brother having such a major operation. Afterward, I couldn't stop thinking about the idea of our hearts growing on their own, creating new vessels when they need to. I wonder if that's what happens when we open ourselves up to love new things, and if so, I know I grew a new vessel this summer for Pakistan and my cousins.

"I miss you, too. Isn't it almost dinnertime there?" I ask. I can tell Zohra is in her bedroom, although it's dim. "Can you turn on the light?"

"We ate already. What are you doing?" Zohra clicks on the lamp by her bed.

"Waking up. I have to get ready for Sunday school in a

minute." Since everyone else was sleeping, I brought a bowl of cereal into the family room and was watching TV while I ate it.

"Why are you wearing lipstick?" I add. Now that I can see the rest of her face more clearly, I notice my cousin's unusually bright lips, along with eyeliner, and blush on her cheeks. "Did you go to a wedding?"

"We had a function at my school this afternoon. For the debate team, and I was the first speaker."

"Like a tournament?"

"Yes." Zohra pumps her fist. "And my team came in second place."

"Nice! Congrats."

"It's so much fun." Zohra wipes her lipstick off with a tissue, and it smears a bit, like clown makeup. "You should try it."

"Debate? No way. I get too nervous when I have to talk in front of an audience."

"Why? What are you scared of?"

"I'm afraid my throat will close up and the words won't

come out," I say, surprised to realize that there are still so many things that Zohra doesn't know about me.

"Come on," Zohra scoffs. "That's not real."

"I'm serious! That's what happens. Every time. I have to push myself to get through it."

"What about singing?" Zohra points an accusing finger at me. "You like to do that, right? Didn't you sing in front of a huge crowd?"

"Yeah, but I was really nervous about it. And that was one time. It's not like I do it every day."

Zohra disappears for a few seconds and then comes back into view with a bowl of pistachios.

"You should join your debate team," she says, chewing.

"No way. And we don't even have one in middle school."

"Well then when you get to secondary school. It's important to know how to speak strongly and convince people of your arguments, Amina."

"I'm good." I pick up my bowl.

"How else are you going to make a difference in the world if you don't use your voice?"

That sounds like something Malala said in her book, and it reminds me that I need to talk to Zohra about my project.

"I need your help with my project and have some questions for you, but I have to go get ready now. Can I call you later on, when it's your morning?"

"Of course." Zohra puckers her clown lips and blows me a kiss. "Ahmed wants to talk to Mustafa. Is he there?"

"Yeah, but he's in the shower. And he has to leave soon too."

"Okay, give my salaams to your parents, and I will talk to you later."

"You too. Give Thaya Jaan an extra big hug from me."

"I will. He gets so happy when I say your name." Zohra laughs without a trace of envy, and I smile through the ache of missing my uncle.

We're going to be late to Sunday school if I don't rush, so I run upstairs and brush my teeth and change while I hear Baba telling Mustafa to hurry.

When I'm ready, I see Thaya Jaan's Quran, the one he

gave me, sitting on my bedside table. Even though I'd still rather be watching TV on the couch than going to Sunday school, I don't dread my Arabic class anymore—thanks to my uncle's patient lessons.

I carefully slip the treasured book into my bag and, after a second thought, add the notebook filled with my lyrics too.

31

Mustafa managed to convince Baba to let him drive us to the Islamic Center. I check my seat belt at least four times and watch as Baba grips the seat so hard his knuckles turn white while Mustafa backs out of the driveway.

"Watch for the mailbox!" Baba warns.

"I know," Mustafa says.

"Slowly, slowly," Baba repeats as we pull out of the neighborhood, and then, as Mustafa passes a parked car, he yells, "Careful!"

Baba reminds me of the way I felt when drivers in Pakistan got so close to bicyclists and other cars that I would alternatively gasp and hold my breath. This ride is stressful too, but mostly because Baba is freaking out.

"Baba, I'm good." Mustafa tries to reassure him as Baba complains that he didn't stop for long enough at the stop sign, that he needs to signal sooner, and that he needs to take his turns tighter.

I'm impressed by Mustafa's calm through it all. Maybe he'll be a decent driver one day.

By the time we arrive at the Islamic Center, Baba's shirt is soaked with sweat. He jumps out of the passenger seat and slips into the driver's side, promising to be back before prayer.

"That was so awesome, right?" Mustafa seems taller than usual as we rush toward the doors to the community hall since we're late for class.

"What was?" I ask.

"Me driving us here. I can't wait to get my license. Then I can bring us alone."

"Oh, right," I agree, now that we're safely here. "Yeah, it was cool. See you."

During break, I search for Rabiya and find her in the

courtyard, eating a plate of biryani that a white-haired uncle is passing out.

"This is so spicy!" she says between bites when she sees me. "It's making my nose run."

"Then why are you eating it?" I ask.

"It's delicious." Rabiya blows her nose. "Want some?"

"No thanks. Is there pizza?"

"I think so."

"I'll get some of that."

Rabiya squints at me since the bright sun is behind me.

"You should go quick before it runs out," she suggests.

"I will, in a minute." I reach into my bag and pull out my notebook, the one she looked at before, as Rabiya continues to eat.

"Listen—" I start to say, but Rabiya puts her plate down on the bench and starts to blow her nose harder and wipe her eyes.

"I'm not crying," she explains. "It's the sun and the spices."

"Listen," I try again. "I wanted to talk to you about this

idea I had. Something I can do to help the new families—something I'm better at than making cards."

Rabiya moves her plate and pats the bench next to her, so I sit down.

"I want to give music lessons to kids who can't afford them," I say. "I'm sure some of the kids who moved here used to take lessons, or want to, and maybe it's hard for their parents to find out where to take them, or to pay for it."

Rabiya doesn't speak and swings her legs on the bench for a moment.

"How would you do it?" she asks.

"I'm not sure yet. I thought we could put up signs here, or maybe our moms could help find kids who would be interested."

"Where would you do it?"

"My house or at their place. Wherever. I can take my keyboard with me if it's somewhere other than my house."

"Did you tell your parents?"

"Of course. They thought it was a good idea and said they would help me. Why? Do you think it isn't?"

"No." Rabiya shakes her head and takes a sip of her lemonade before continuing. "It's an amazing idea. Why didn't I think of it?"

"You're not mad that I don't want to do the cards?" I ask.

"Totally not. I mean, I've seen your art. No offense." Rabiya laughs.

"It's okay." I smile, relieved. "Do you think you can help me make me a couple cool signs to put up with sign-up sheets on the bulletin boards?"

"Sure. Like the ones with the tear-off phone number things?"

"Yeah. And"—I hand her my notebook, with the word "PRIVATE" facing up—"I thought about it, and I *do* want you to read this. All of it."

"Really?" Rabiya takes the notebook from me carefully, like it's made out of glass, and her eyes grow wider.

"You know me better than anyone. And if I am having an identity crisis, at least you can help me get a good song out of it."

"Are you sure?" Rabiya looks sheepish. "I told my mom I asked you about the identity crisis thing, and she was mad at me for talking about things she says I don't understand. She said you're doing fine, for a teenager."

"Well that's nice. I think."

"Are you fine?"

"I think so. I'm figuring things out. But that's okay. Like my dad says, the world is messy and complicated."

"Okay." Rabiya pats the notebook in her lap. "I hope your lyrics won't make me cry or anything. I've already used up all my napkins."

"I think you'll be okay." I put my arm around her and squeeze. "You're tough."

"Thanks, Amina." Rabiya smiles at me and wipes her nose again. There's no time left for pizza, but I'm glad that I got to talk to her. No matter how much I love Zohra, Rabiya has been the closest thing to a sister that I've had for as long as I can remember. And I need her to know she matters.

"I missed you while I was in Pakistan. A lot. I'm sorry I've been acting weird," I say.

"It's okay. I missed you, too." Rabiya's big brown eyes shine as she flips open my notebook and starts to read.

32

Ms. Holly sings a bunch of nonsense words in a falsetto while she moves her head from side to side like a chicken.

Nico turns to me with his mouth twisting in all kinds of directions, and I stifle a laugh.

"Cheep, cheep, cheep," she concludes, waving her head and hands back and forth. We're seated in a circle on the stage, and she is putting on an unexpected show for the drama club.

"Okay, and then the boys chime in with 'Good night, ladies.' It's a round." Ms. Holly beams. "Can you remember the words and try it?"

Now everyone starts to laugh for real.

"What is *that*?" Julie asks.

"It's from *The Music Man*, only my favorite show ever. I thought we could practice some of the songs, and if you all like it, maybe it could be the choice for the spring musical."

"Isn't that a bit, I don't know, old-fashioned?" Julie asks as she scans the room, checking to see who agrees with her.

"Maybe. But it's got everything." Ms. Holly clutches her chest. "Romance, intrigue, friendship, redemption."

She walks over to her computer, which is plugged into a speaker, and hits a button.

"Listen to this," she says.

A syrupy sweet voice starts belting out a ballad, singing to her love, to her "someone." We all listen politely.

"Isn't that fantastic?" Ms. Holly asks. "This was the first production I was ever in, back when I was in sixth grade, and I've loved it ever since. We'll sing the songs in class tomorrow."

"I think we should do something from this century," Nico whispers to me as we break and move to grab our things from the wall.

"Amina." Ms. Holly stops me as we walk by her. "I think you could make a wonderful Marian."

"Who?"

"The female lead. You could sing her songs beautifully. Like the one we heard."

"Oh. Um. Thanks. But I don't know." Ms. Holly may have been the reason I stood up to sing one song at the recital, but starring in a musical and acting is something I never see myself doing.

Ms. Holly smiles in the way she does that means she thinks she knows something that I don't.

"We'll have auditions after winter break. Just something to think about, hon."

"I will."

"You wouldn't want to?" Nico asks me as we walk away.

"I don't know. I get super nervous onstage when everyone is staring at me. And I don't think I'd be a good actor."

"You can be good at anything you want." Nico shakes his head. "You can't think like that."

"I guess." I shrug.

Nico stops walking and puts his hand on my arm. His eyes are so intense that the little flecks are practically glowing.

"We both know I'm not the best producer in the world. But I keep trying, right?"

"Yeah."

"I try because I like the feeling of creating something new. And the idea of someone else getting it."

"I know." I mean it. I honestly do.

"And you love singing, right? Is that only for you, or do you dream about singing for others?" Nico is forcing me to share the things I often think about but don't usually talk about.

"Well, both," I admit. The truth is I used to dream of being on *The Voice*, and I've imagined what it would be like to hear a song of my own on the radio. But I never thought any of that could actually happen. Not even after singing onstage last year.

"Then don't be afraid. You have to put yourself out there, Amina, and do you. Unless . . . Marian is a dancer. In that case, skip it for sure."

"Very funny," I laugh as I push his hand away. "But thanks."

"Well, I also need you to do something for me. Are you ready to sing that hook?"

I don't tell Nico that I've been practicing it.

"Yeah," I say. "And then maybe you can help me produce my song? I think I'm almost ready for that, too."

Nico's eyes widen, and his smile grows bigger. "For sure."

33

I clutch the bag that contains my props, including my headscarf. It's hard to believe that I'm walking through the school hallways wearing a shalwar kameez, and it wasn't my mother's idea.

This one happens to be my favorite. Its vibrant turquoise-blue kameez is decorated with delicate red embroidery around the neckline and wrists. The long scarf I'm wearing with it is a cheerful red with a blue border.

Today I don't get a second look for being dressed this way. The halls are filled with seventh graders wearing white coats, army fatigues, dashikis, and a kimono. That's because the week of our Living Wax Museum projects is finally here.

We've been presenting to our classrooms since yesterday, and this evening is the school-wide program when we perform for everyone, including our families and friends.

I spent an hour last night rehearsing, after Baba helped me work on my speech. Mama suggested I practice in front of the family, but I was too nervous to bust out in my accent in front of them. Plus, I was certain that if Mustafa was around, we'd both start to crack up, and I'd never get through it. Instead I practiced in front of the mirror alone in my room. It helped me relax to hold an old Harry Potter wand I use as a fake microphone when I sing in private.

By the time I walk into history class, though, all that preparation feels like a total waste. Nervousness is bubbling up inside me like the can of Sprite an eighth grader shook at lunch and tried to offer everyone. I'm afraid I'm going to explode.

"Hey, Amina," Briana calls out to me. "I like your outfit."

"Thanks. I like yours, too," I say, careful not to make eye contact with Sheila or her friends as I slide into my seat. I don't want to give anyone the chance to comment on anything about me, my clothes, or what else about Malala makes them feel sad today.

Briana is dressed like the astronaut Sally Ride and has a jumpsuit covered with homemade patches that say NASA. I'm pretty sure she's holding a plastic punch bowl for a helmet.

Mr. Griffiths had us pick numbers to decide the order for our presentations. I ended up on day two. Each of us has exactly five minutes to speak, and Mr. Griffiths has a timer that we have to press when we start. Five minutes doesn't sound like a whole lot, unless you hate public speaking. In that case, it's an eternity. When we're done, we have to answer a few questions.

"Okay, class, you know the drill. Let's get started right away so we can get through the rest of you today. Who's up first?"

"Me." Kevin stands and moves to the front. He's dressed in a suit and wearing a fake mustache as he presents as Langston Hughes. And in a stroke of genius, Kevin holds up lines of his poems on large white cards as he speaks about the writer's life. Everyone is moved.

"Brilliant." Mr. Griffiths claps. "That was wonderful. Who has a question?"

Kevin stays in character as he answers a few basic questions about Langston Hughes's life. I'm too jumpy to ask a question, and I keep checking my bag to make sure everything I need is there.

The next four presenters go by in a blur as I recite my lines in my head. We have Mother Teresa, Galileo, Nelson Mandela, and Steve Jobs. And then it's my turn to go.

I pull my red scarf out of my bag and carefully drape it over my head, leaving the front of my hair visible, like Malala. And then I stand as straight as I can and walk to the front of the room.

You got through this before. You can do this, too.

"I am Malala Yousafzai," I say in the accent I practiced after watching her speeches countless times. "I am a fearless fighter for girls' education who overcame a horrific attempt to silence me."

I exhale and continue to say a few more words about Malala and her incredibly journey, her fund and efforts to promote education, and her first visit back to her country. As I speak, I remember to look into the audience, and I pick a few friendly faces to focus on, including Briana's.

"I might be the only Pakistani woman you've ever heard of before, but there are so many other women from my country who are just as important to know about too . . . like someone who inspired me."

I quickly pull off my scarf and replace it with a thin white one.

"I am Benazir Bhutto, and I was elected prime minister of Pakistan twice, the first time in 1988. I was the female head of a democratic state before many western countries had ever achieved this, including the United States."

The friendly faces are a bit confused now, and I avoid glancing at Mr. Griffiths as I continue speaking.

I whip off the scarf and put on a ski hat and some goggles.

"I'm Samina Baig, a Pakistani mountaineer. I climbed all seven of the highest peaks in the world, including Mount Everest, in fourteen months, when I was only twenty-three years old. I like to say that if a girl can climb the highest mountains, she can do anything with hard work, passion, commitment, and encouragement."

I hear a few murmurs from the class, and someone whistles and says "awesome" under his breath as I remove the ski mask and goggles and replace them with a pair of aviator sunglasses.

"I am Ayesha Farooq, and I'm Pakistan's first female fighter pilot. I scored the highest possible marks on my air force exam, and I say instead of looking up to role models, be one yourself."

I'm startled as a few people start to clap, and I check the timer. I only have thirty seconds left, so I quickly pull out a photo I enlarged of Zohra standing next to me, dressed up for a party, making a silly face.

"I am Zohra Khokar, and I am a sixteen-year-old student at the Lahore Grammar School in Lahore, Pakistan. I'm fortunate to have a comfortable life and love watching movies, debating, and swimming. I'm studying hard and want to be a future leader. I'm proud to be a Pakistani, and

I hope you'll think of people like me when you think of my country."

I put the photo down, and the class erupts into applause. A bunch of hands shoot up, and I take a deep breath and answer a few questions, mostly about Samina Baig.

"Okay, class, we need to move on." Mr. Griffiths raises his hand last. "See me after class," he adds as he gives me a long stare.

34

I approach Mr. Griffiths with dread, ready to get a lecture or, worse, a failing grade.

"Amina, you understand your presentation falls outside the parameters of the assignment," Mr. Griffiths starts to say, pushing up his glasses and sounding exasperated. "The ones we spent a lot of time establishing as a department."

I remain silent.

"I enjoyed reading your assignments on Malala. And you had a strong research update. Can you please explain why you decided to change things without letting me know?"

I gulp, unsure what to say, but then decide to go with the truth.

"After my presentation, people said things like how they felt sad that girls don't have rights in Pakistan—" I stop when Mr. Griffiths frowns.

"Continue," he urges.

"And that they're so lucky they don't live there."

"I see." Mr. Griffiths's frown grows bigger, and I decide to plead my case after all.

"I was in Pakistan this summer, and my family lives there, and many other women in Pakistan have done great things, other than Malala. And though she's an incredible person, most of the time she's the only Pakistani people have ever heard of, and it makes them feel sorry for everyone else and think that bad things like that are the only things that happen there, but they shouldn't."

Mr. Griffiths holds up his hand, like a cop stopping traffic, but I continue.

"I was going to ask if I could switch to do my project on someone else but thought it was too late, and then I had this idea. I'm sorry I didn't follow the rules, and I know it might hurt my grade." I rush to get all the words in.

Mr. Griffiths sighs.

"I didn't hear those conversations as they were happening," he says. "I think you learned, and taught your classmates, an important lesson. But I have to think about how this will impact your evaluation. There have to be consequences for not following instructions."

"Okay," I say. That seems fair enough. But I don't regret my choice one bit.

Mr. Griffiths shakes his head as I go toward the door, and I can't tell if it's out of disappointment or annoyance that I'm making his job harder. But when I reach the doorway, he adds, "Your presentation took courage, Amina. I bet Malala would appreciate your message."

I nod, hoping that means he'll go easy on me, and leave the room.

Several hours later, I'm in my Malala outfit again in the cafeteria for the main event and have already presented to a bunch of groups of people who've come by. I'm frozen until someone presses a pretend button on the table near me that makes me "come to life." Then I share my prepared statement in character and answer questions.

It's tiring switching my costume each time I present, but I'm much more relaxed now than I was during class. Talking to small groups of people is easier than standing in front of a room of kids staring at me. And only a trickle of latecomers are left.

The atmosphere in the cafeteria is festive, with two long tables filled with snacks that parent volunteers brought. Some tried to be creative and link the treat to their kids' historical figures, like "Newton's apples," and there's a cake shaped like a boulder that says HISTORY ROCKS.

The jumbo aluminum tray of veggie samosas Mama bought from the gray-haired man who owns our local Indian grocery store is almost empty. But the sweet jalebis are almost untouched. Most people don't know what to make of the bright orange tangled mess of sticky treats. I take a break, help myself to a big one, and try not to let the syrup drip on my clothes as I munch on it and wait for the next group of people to approach me.

Mr. Griffiths is wandering around the cafeteria, talking to some of the adults, peering at the snacks but not eating any, and as he catches my eye as I'm stuffing the rest of my jalebi in my mouth instead of remaining a statue, he gives me an awkward little salute. I have a feeling he'll go easy on me with my grade.

Soojin has a crowd of people around her and is an animated Ada Lovelace, although the way she is waving her arms around makes her look like she's dancing more than programming a computer. Emily is on the other side of me. She decided to be Ruth Bader Ginsburg, which made her mom super happy. She's wearing a black graduation gown with a white collar sticking out, and her hair is in a tight bun with powder on it to make it gray. When the people around her move on, she smiles and waves to me with the meat mallet she is using as a gavel.

"Thirsty?" Mustafa hands me a cup of water after spending the last half hour circling the room, saying hi to his old teachers and catching up with a few friends who are also here with their younger siblings.

"Thanks." I grab the water and chug it.

"Baba is torturing some poor kid who is Elon Musk over there." Mustafa grins, and I notice his usually scruffy beard is neatly trimmed today. He looks nice, and like a grown man compared to the middle schoolers in the room. "He's asking him all these supertechnical science questions."

"That's so Baba," I laugh.

"Ma and Mrs. Park are watching Frida Kahlo. She's actually painting live."

"That girl's an amazing artist. She's going to be famous for real one day."

"I saw Nico over there as Mozart. I like the wig. But I thought he was George Washington."

"I did too at first."

"People are talking about your presentation," Mustafa says.

"Really?"

"I overheard them. They said you made them think about things they hadn't considered before. And that it was clever."

"Are you sure they were talking about me?" I want to believe my brother, but it's surprising to hear that people would have anything to say about my presentation when there's Langston Hughes reciting poetry and a live art demonstration.

"I don't see any other Malala in here. It's you, Amina. Be proud of yourself. You did good."

"Thanks." I smile at Mustafa.

Then, as he turns toward the food table, my brother adds, "But don't let your head get too big for that scarf."

And that's how I know that even if he almost looks like a man, and even if he drove us here tonight, he's still Mustafa.

35

"You were fantastic." Mama pulls my covers over me and sits down on the edge of the bed.

"Thanks, Mama." Ever since I started middle school, my parents don't often come into my room to tuck me in at night, but I love it when they do. "I hope Mr. Griffiths doesn't give me a bad grade."

"You should get extra credit. You did all that research on those other women. I hadn't heard of a couple of them."

"Zohra helped. I just sent her a long message thanking her."

"Well, no matter what grade you get, we're proud of you. And I know Thaya Jaan will be too. Did you send him the video Baba took tonight?"

My pulse quickens as I imagine Thaya Jaan listening to my fake accent and imitating real Pakistani heroes. But I will send the video. He's going into surgery in two days, and maybe watching it will help keep his mind off of it. And I hope he's happy that I'm trying to keep the promise I made him.

"I met Nico's mom tonight," Mama says.

Uh-oh.

"She's nice," Mama continues. "Her parents still live in Egypt, and her husband is French. They met when he was studying in Cairo."

"I know. Nico told me."

"I didn't ask if they are Muslim, or say anything to embarrass you, in case you're wondering."

"Nico already told me he's both Muslim and Christian."

"Oh." Mama smiles and reaches over to push the hair out of my face. "Mrs. Bertrand said she's glad to see you and Nico become friends, because he wasn't thrilled about moving here, and it isn't easy for him to meet new people."

"He has other friends."

"Well, I guess none of them are as nice as you." Mama's eyes are soft, and her hand lingers on my cheek. "I thought about what you said the other day and talked to your father about it." She clears her throat. "It's okay for the two of you to be friends, as long as you're always open and honest with us about everything. Is that fair?"

"Yup." I try to stay calm, even though it's weirding me out to imagine my parents having that conversation.

"And you're sure that Nico wants nothing more than friendship with you?"

I want to stop talking about this but force myself to think about what Mama is asking. Nothing Nico has ever said or done has been anything other than friendly. And I've never felt uncomfortable or thought he felt anything romantic toward me. The only thoughts like that that have crossed my mind are because of other people's reactions and questions.

"Yeah. I'm sure," I finally reply. It's true. I honestly am, and I find it oddly comforting.

"You'll let me know if that changes in any way, right?"

"I promise."

Mama sits quietly for a while, and her voice catches when she speaks again. "I don't know how you grew up so fast. You know you'll always be my sweet baby girl, right?"

"I know." I take Mama's hand and squeeze it. "And, Mama, Nico and I talked about it, and he wants to help me with the music lessons for kids. And with recording a song. Is that okay?"

"It's okay with me. And that reminds me, we might have a first student for your lessons, a little girl named Aisha. Her mother was inquiring at the Islamic Center."

"Really? How old is she?"

"I think she's seven or eight, quite musical, and she loves the piano, just like you."

"That's so awesome!" I can't wait to meet her, and I wonder what it will be like to have someone older than Sumaiya to teach.

Mama leans over and kisses me.

"I'm proud of you, but don't grow up too quick," she says. "Love you."

"Love you, too, Mama."

Mama stands up and heads out of the room.

"Should I turn off the light?" she asks.

"I'll do it in a bit."

After Mama leaves, I pick up Thaya Jaan's Quran from my side table. I read a few verses from it and then make a special dua for him. I ask God to make his surgery go smoothly, and for him to get better soon.

Next, I pick up my notebook and flip it open. Rabiya and I talked about my lyrics the other day, but I haven't had a chance to work on them since then. All evening at school, my mind was filled with words bouncing around in my head like the popcorn machine someone had set up in the corner of the cafeteria.

I pour them out on the page and don't stop until the last sentence has captured every emotion I've been struggling to express.

36

"What are we supposed to call you now?" I ask Soojin.

"Um, how about . . . Soojin?" Soojin looks confused. "It's not like I changed my name or anything."

"You don't prefer Madam President?" Emily asks.

"Or Your Excellency?" I add with a grin.

"Oh, that's what you mean!" Soojin laughs. "I like the sound of Madam President."

"Okay then," I say. "It's official."

"I still can't believe I won, though," Soojin adds. "You two are the best campaign managers ever!"

"We know." Emily puts her arm around me. "I couldn't believe it either when Mr. Little read off the winners' names at dismissal. I mean, I believed it, but, you know, I was surprised! You did it!"

"*We* did it." Soojin beams. "I didn't even hear my name because everyone in seventh period started cheering, and I had to ask someone who won. I was sure it was Julie."

"I knew you were going to win," I say. "You had to."

We're sitting at a table at Soojin's family's restaurant. Mrs. Park said she'd pick us up from school and take us out to celebrate the election results after Soojin called her to tell her the good news. But instead of Kopp's this time, we all asked to come here. Mrs. Park gave us some delicious spicy soy garlic chicken bites to start with, and I ordered the kimbap. It's like a giant sushi roll, but with different fillings. Mr. Park makes them at home with pieces of their famous bulgogi inside, and last time I was over, we convinced him to add it to the menu.

"It's because of you, Amina," Soojin adds, after taking a bite of chicken. "I think your idea got people to pay attention to me."

"I was just doing my job," I say. But I can't help feeling

proud of the way Soojin's campaign came together. Once we decided to focus on service, Soojin made that the center of her platform. We came up with slogans like "We Can Do Better" and "Put the 'U' in Community" and hung sign-up sheets for different service opportunities. I was pleasantly surprised when a bunch of kids added their names to volunteer for apartment setups and helping with free music lessons and tutoring for kids. Emily added activities like working with a food pantry and kitchen, and she even got the auntie who makes shami kabobs to pitch in and donate food.

In the end, we did manage to make Soojin's campaign stand out, especially compared to Julie, whose slogans were "Vote for the Best" and "Join Julie's Jewels." Her face was plastered on all her campaign materials, along with lots of sparkly stickers and glitter.

"So many people signed up," Emily says. "Is there such a thing as too many volunteers?"

Soojin and I look at each other, and she shrugs.

"I don't think so, right? We'll figure it out."

Emily looks at her phone.

"My mom says congratulations. She's so glad I was working hard on this that last night she said I can focus on whatever clubs I want."

"Are you quitting chess, then?" I ask.

"I don't know yet." Emily reaches for another piece of chicken. "I mean, chess is cool and all, but I'm not as into it as the other kids are, or as good as them, and I don't want to compete or anything."

"I feel you." I nod. "You have to do you."

"You sound exactly like Nico," Soojin laughs.

"Yikes. I do, don't I?" I giggle. "I'm spending way too much time with him lately."

"Too much, huh?" Soojin takes a sip of her drink and winks at Emily.

"Are you sure you don't mean 'not enough'?" Emily jumps in and gives me a side-eye.

"Here you go, girls." Mrs. Park interrupts us and puts our food down in front of us. My kimbap is beautiful, sliced into neat disks that I can't wait to devour.

"Enjoy." She smiles at us. "We sold a lot of these at lunch today."

"Thank you for the suggestion," Mr. Park yells from behind the counter. "You get a lifelong free supply."

He's kidding, because the Parks already refuse to take any money from us, no matter how hard we or our parents try to pay for meals when we come in.

As Mrs. Park walks away, I look at my friends, who are still staring at me, which means they aren't done talking about Nico yet.

"Nico's great and all. But you're still my best friends."

"And?" Soojin asks.

"And I can never spend enough time with you."

Soojin nods her head with approval, and Emily sighs with exaggerated relief.

"Good answer," she says.

We all smile, and then dig into our food.

37

“Don’t laugh,” I say, and I hand Nico the notebook. He’s perched at the kitchen table on Saturday afternoon, and the sun is streaming through the window.

He reaches his hand out, and I pull the notebook back instead of giving it to him.

“Promise first,” I insist.

Nico puts a hand over his heart like he’s about to say the Pledge of Allegiance, although his hair is covering his eyes, and I can’t properly see them.

“I solemnly swear.”

“Okay, here.”

I hand him the notebook, help him find the right page,

and then pace back and forth in our kitchen while he reads. It's forever before he speaks.

"I'm done—you can sit down now," Nico says.

"And?"

"And, well . . ." He hesitates. "Do you want me to be completely honest?"

"Yes." My heart pounds in my ears.

"It's . . . almost perfect."

I can't tell if he's being serious or not.

"Are you just saying that?" I ask.

"No."

I exhale slowly and notice I'm sweating.

"So, what's wrong with it?"

"Nothing. But I don't know what this means." Nico points to a line in the song.

"That's Punjabi. It means 'my heart isn't connected without you.'"

"Can you say that again?"

"My heart isn't connected without you."

Nico writes the words down after the Punjabi with

a pencil. "I think if you repeat the line in English, right here"—Nico pushes his hair out of his face, and I see his eyes are sincere—"it's pretty much perfect."

"You really like it?" I feel a rush of relief and giddiness.

"Yeah. It's the stuff we've been talking about, things you've been thinking of. You nailed it."

"Thank you."

"I think a lot of people will connect to your words."

I hope so.

"So, what's next?" I ask.

"Now you sing it. I have this—" Nico pulls out a microphone that is shaped like a softball on a tripod. "My uncle let me borrow it. It won't be professional quality if we do it here instead of at a recording studio, but it'll be good enough. Who knows, maybe enough to get a record label interested."

"Yeah, right. I wish." I act confident as my insides quiver at the idea of recording myself singing my words.

Nico opens up his laptop, and I see the green boxes, which have become more familiar to me now. He's been working on the beat we started together and sending me clips to listen to, and it's almost complete. But I think it needs a little more.

"Can we add some tabla and harmonium to it, like in the qawali songs I played for you?"

"I was waiting for you to ask, and I got you." Nico slips on his headphones. Then he reaches into his bag and pulls out a splitter. "Where are your headphones?"

Baba comes into the kitchen singing loudly in his extra-deep baritone, but he stops mid-note when he sees us at work.

"Oh, sorry." He grins. "I thought you might need a backup singer."

"I think we're okay, Mr. Khokar." Nico smiles.

"Want something to eat?" Baba asks. "Amina's mom made some chocolate chip cookies."

"Sure." Nico reaches into the tin Baba holds in front of him, takes a short stack of cookies, and puts them on a napkin in front of him.

"Milk?" Baba asks.

"That would be great."

"What about you, Amina?"

"No thanks." I can't eat right now, and while I appreciate Baba's hospitality, I would also like him to hurry up and leave so I can finally sing this song, before I chicken out.

I'm glad to see Baba joking around again, and I know it's because Thaya Jaan's surgery went smoothly yesterday and he's recovering in the hospital. Baba came into my room late last night after he spoke to the surgeon and woke me up like I made him swear to do. He whispered the news to me, gave me a big kiss, and left to say prayers of thanks. I fell back asleep and slept more peacefully than I have in weeks. Thaya Jaan is going to have to stay at the hospital for a few days, and I can't wait to talk to him when he gets home.

Baba is barely out the door when Mustafa wanders in.

"Baba said there are cookies?" he asks.

"Here." Nico hands Mustafa the tin, which Baba left on the table.

"How's it going?" Mustafa inhales a cookie.

"Fine," I say, "except we keep getting interrupted."

Mustafa doesn't take the hint and sits down next to Nico instead. He picks up my notebook and puts on the headphones I took out of my bag.

Nico turns to me and shrugs. "I guess this is turning into a family project?"

"Welcome to the family." Mustafa grins and hands him a cookie. "Need my help? I can sing backup."

"Baba already offered," I say.

"Okay, but you're missing out on my amazing vocals. Where do you think you get it from? Clearly not our father."

"Is he serious?" Nico looks at me, confused.

"No." I roll my eyes.

"I think Amina's going to go solo," Nico says. "But do you want to help with the video? Amina said you take amazing photos."

"I'm all right," Mustafa says.

"Cool," Nico says.

I can't tell if everyone is excited about our project or trying to keep tabs on us. But either way, they need to let us get on with it.

"Okay, can you please go now so we can record?" I plead.

"Sure. Although you might want to go downstairs so you don't catch those mowers outside. Or Mr. Nelson's dog barking," Mustafa suggests.

"Should we go downstairs?" Nico asks.

"Let's practice one time here first," I say.

I'm finally ready to sing this and can't wait a moment longer.

38

"You're going to be so famous."

The lyrics may not be perfect, like Nico claims, but they're mine. And the recording isn't professional, but it's pretty close. I hit all my notes and sound like I know what I'm doing. But if I listened to Rabiya, I'd be convinced I'm going to win a Grammy.

"It's amazing! You're, like, amazing! I can't believe you did this all by yourselves."

Rabiya is almost jumping with excitement, her body a blur of limbs moving in different directions as she speaks.

"Did everyone see this? Did your friends see it?" Rabiya continues. "Who made the video?"

"We all did. Nico and Mustafa helped, but mostly me."

"Mustafa helped?"

"Yeah, he totally wanted to. He took some of the new footage."

"I want to see it again." Rabiya picks up my phone and presses play. I lean against her and watch over her shoulder.

The song starts with shots of our neighborhood, then it moves from our quiet street, to Southridge Mall, the Islamic Center, and outside my school. You see the back of me walking with my friends, wearing my backpack and headphones. And then it switches to scenes of me walking in the chaotic streets of Lahore, the colorful market, and the majestic Wazir Khan Mosque. The video weaves scenes from both parts of my life as you hear the track and my singing over it. My favorite part is when the camera pans around the room at Thaya Jaan's when we're drinking chai.

"It's so awesome," Rabiya whispers as it plays. "It's going to be huge. When are you putting it on YouTube?"

"I don't know. I want to, but I'm scared."

"You have to." Rabiya turns to me, and her eyes are gigantic. "Come on!"

"I'm nervous to have it out there." I'm not talking about the technical aspects. Mustafa had a conversation with my parents earlier, asking for their permission to post it. He showed them other examples, and they decided that as long as we disabled comments and didn't have any way for people to find out personal information about me, it was okay with them.

Instead, I've got the same jitters I had when Nico read my lyrics for the first time: How will people react? Will they get it? Will they appreciate the different aspects of my life and understand how they're all important to me? And will they see the Pakistan that I see?

"You have to share it," Rabiya repeats. "Why would you put so much work into this, if you don't want people to see it?"

I bite my lip.

"Ms. Holly offered to let me upload it to the drama club YouTube channel," I say.

"That's perfect. Are you going to?"

"Maybe."

Rabiya grabs my hand and starts to jump for real this time.

"Do it!" she cheers. "Who knows who might listen to it! What if you get discovered?"

"I want to do something else first," I say.

I take a deep breath, press a button, and send the file to Zohra over WhatsApp, with the message I hope you all like this. ♥

A few minutes later, the phone buzzes. It's Zohra. When I pick up, I'm moved by the emotion in her face, from more than seven thousand miles away.

"I don't know what to say." Zohra's eyes are brimming with tears. "This is so beautiful, Amina. I'm blown away. Your voice is gorgeous. And the song—"

"Thank you," I interrupt, because her praise is making me uncomfortable. I blink fast—seeing her reaction is making my eyes fill up too.

Zohra smiles. "I have a surprise for you!"

She flips the camera, and I see the family room, Thaya

Jaan's favorite chair, and the hallway to his bedroom. Then she walks down the hall and into Thaya Jaan's room. He's in bed, reclining against pillows, and I can't tell if he's awake or asleep.

"Don't disturb him," I say, afraid to see him up close.

"It's okay, he's awake. Abu, it's Amina."

Thaya Jaan looks frail, and his hair and beard are uncharacteristically messy. When he sees me in the phone, he waves slightly but doesn't speak. My throat tightens as I see this altered version of my uncle lying there.

"She has something special to show you." Zohra continues to chirp like there's nothing unusual about the way Thaya Jaan looks or his slow movements. "Watch."

Zohra hands him a tablet and plays my video on it. I hear my voice as the song plays and hold my breath as my uncle stares at the video in silence. When the last notes of the song end, my insides are about to burst. I can't read his face and worry that he finds it foolish or weird.

Thaya Jaan shakes his head slightly, and Zohra moves the tablet away. Then my uncle raises his hand to his heart, and a mini version of his smile slowly appears on his face.

"Masha'Allah, Abu! Amina, this is the first time he's smiled since the surgery!" Zohra cheers.

As I exhale, Thaya Jaan motions for her to bring the phone closer. I look into his eyes, which are tired but resolute, and I know he's still fighting for all of us.

"We love you, Thaya Jaan." I blow him a kiss.

Zohra smooths the blanket over her father and leaves the room. Her face is bright as she turns the camera back to herself.

"He watched the video you sent a million times. It was all he talked about the day before the operation. I know we are going to be hearing this song a lot too."

"He's going to be okay, right? Why isn't he talking?"

"He's really hoarse from the surgery, so it hurts for him to speak. But don't worry, the doctors say he's doing well. And it helps that he has all your love and prayers."

The tears I've been holding back start to roll down my face as my cousin says that, but not because I'm sad. I'm grateful—to have her, Thaya Jaan, my family, and friends in my life, both in Pakistan and here at home. All of them are pieces of me. And that makes them part of my song, the song of my heart.

"So, when's the tour?" Zohra asks. "And the album?"

"I know, right?" Rabiya yells from behind me.

"Who's that?" Zohra laughs.

"It's Rabiya," I say. "Here, say hi."

As I hand off the phone, the two start to plan my tour and my next video, and crack jokes about my musical taste. I listen to them and make a wish that they get the chance to meet in person one day soon. And then, inspired by the sound of their laughter and by this moment, I quickly log in to the YouTube account Ms. Holly gave me.

Maybe my heart had to ache while it grew to make room for all the people and places I love. But it was worth it. I know there are many others like me, who are trying to figure out where they belong, make sense of our complicated and wonderful world, and get other people to care. So, after my finger hovers over the button for a moment, I hold my breath and hit upload, sending my song out there for everyone who needs it.

ACKNOWLEDGMENTS

The outpouring of love and support for *Amina's Voice* was far beyond my wildest dreams, and was what led me to write this sequel, something I had secretly hoped for when I first imagined Amina's story. Thank you to everyone who has shared thoughts or ideas with me since its publication. I incorporated many of your suggestions and am incredibly grateful for all of them.

This book wouldn't be possible without my agent, Matthew Elblonk, seeing the potential in Amina's story when it was in rough form. You're the best, Matthew, for helping me navigate publishing ever since.

Zareen Jaffery championed Amina from the outset and launched her into the world, along with a new imprint. Zareen, you loved my characters as much as I do and empowered me to tell the stories I believe in, without compromise. I'm forever indebted.

Kendra Levin helped me complete this book and gently guided it to a satisfying place. It's stronger because of your thoughtful input, Kendra. And to everyone in the Simon & Schuster/Salaam Reads family, a huge thank-you for all that you do to bring my books to life and launch them.

I'm in awe of Abigail Dela Cruz's incredible cover art. Thank you for attracting readers through the sheer beauty of your work.

Once again, my writing group came through for me with wonderful feedback and suggestions for this story. Laura Gehl, Joan Waites, and Ann McCallum—you are my trusted sounding board.

N. H. Senzai was generous with her time and talent. Naheed, you know Amina wouldn't exist without you.

Naya Shams offered me a teen perspective and deeply understood Amina's character. You are tremendously perceptive and wise beyond your years, Naya. I also appreciate your insightful mom, Amina Maryem Shams, for helping me pinpoint the feelings I wanted to capture in her namesake character.

My dear cousin Amna Burki was kind enough to read my draft with extra attention to the Pakistani perspective.

Amna, you are my Zohra, and I appreciate your open-mindedness, sensitivity, and storytelling instincts.

Afgen Sheikh is a smart and valuable friend who always helps make my stories better and funnier. Thank you for your honest critique—I left out "tunes" this time.

My sister, Andala, is my biggest promoter and loves my stories almost as much as she loves me. Thanks, sis, for being an important part of this process.

Bilal, my older son, coached me on music production and is the inspiration behind Amina's gift, along with being a speedy reviewer over the years. My younger son, Humza, supplies me with encouragement and the greatest hugs, and reminds me why this work matters. And my husband, Farrukh, is the one who believes in me when I don't, cheerleads when I'm down, and thinks every book is better than the last. I hope you're right, and I love you all more than anything.

My mother and father are the reason I'm a writer, and why I write about love in its many forms. I can never thank you both enough for teaching me to have pride in who I am, and for seeing the good in the world, no matter how messy and complicated it is.

And, finally, my readers are amazing and make it possible for me to keep telling stories. My heart keeps growing to make room for you.

READING GROUP GUIDE FOR

Amina's Song

by Hena Khan

About the Book

Amina's Song picks up after *Amina's Voice* leaves off; these books can be read in any order as companion novels. As Amina prepares to enter seventh grade, she becomes more aware of navigating her dual identities as an American and a Pakistani girl. A summer trip to visit her uncle Thaya Jaan and extended family in Pakistan opens her eyes to the rich culture of her family's homeland, sparking a desire to share her culture with her friends and classmates in America and to counter stereotypes. Music provides the answer that she's looking for, but this time around, she won't use her voice to sing a song written by someone else; with the help of her new friend Nico, she will share her own unique song with the world.

Discussion Questions

1. Before you begin reading, brainstorm everything you know or think you know about the country of Pakistan. Next, make a list of things you want to know about Pakistan. After you finish reading, look back at your list. Were the things you believed you knew correct? What did you learn about Pakistan by reading *Amina's Song*? What are you still curious to know?

2. Why was Amina initially nervous about visiting Pakistan? Explain how her experience in Pakistan was different from what she expected.

3. Amina remembers her father explaining the difference between rational and irrational fear. Why is it important to recognize this distinction? How can you tell the difference? Can you give examples from your own experiences or from the novel?

4. Why does Amina want her classmates and friends in America to see Pakistan the way she sees it? Why is she happy when she learns that America is helping to preserve a World Heritage Site in Pakistan?

5. Why do you think Amina is emotional when it comes time for her visit to Pakistan to end? Can you relate to how Amina feels when she says goodbye to her uncle, aunts, and cousins? What experience of your own comes to mind?

6. Amina and her cousin Zohra have very different approaches to bargaining with the street vendors at the market in Pakistan. Describe the differences in the ways they approach their roles as customers. Do you think you would be more like Zohra or Amina in a similar situation?

7. Explain how seeing the little boy asking for money in Pakistan impacts Amina. How does she turn this sense of empathy into action to help others once she returns to America?

8. When she is on the plane returning to the United States, Amina wonders if her brother is "as mixed up as I am, as we travel not only through time zones but also from one part of our lives to another." Why does leaving Pakistan cause her to feel this way? Do you have a place that is so important to you that it feels like it is a part of you? Explain your answers.

9. Why does Soojin decide to run for student body president? What sets her campaign apart from her competitors? Have you ever considered running for student government? Explain your answers.

10. What does Amina realize about Rabiya's feelings toward her friendship with Zohra and her trip to Pakistan? What do you think might have happened if Amina had gotten angry with Rabiya instead of considering how Rabiya might be feeling? What actions does she take instead, and how does her response toward Rabiya impact their relationship?

11. Toward the end of the book, Amina reflects, "even if my friends can't understand everything I've been going through lately, they're trying. And we can support each other while we do different things." What steps does Amina take to maintain her friendships with Emily and Soojin? Why do you think some friends grow apart while others remain? Can you learn anything from Amina, Soojin, and Emily about how to be a good friend?

12. Why does Amina choose to research Malala for her history project? Explain why sharing her preliminary research makes Amina worry that she's chosen the wrong person to profile. How does Amina solve this dilemma? Why do you think her teacher calls her decision "brave"?

13. All the seventh-grade students participate in a Living Wax Museum project, where they research, dress as, and present reports on a historical figure. You may have participated in a similar project in the past. If so, whom did you choose as your historical figure? Reflect on your reasons for selecting them and what you learned. If you have never participated in this activity, whom would you select to research and impersonate? Why would you choose them?

14. One of Amina's strengths is her ability to consider what other people might be thinking or experiencing and how they might feel. Read the last paragraphs of chapter eleven. What can you learn from Amina's example? How does having and practicing empathy change the way a person interacts with other people?

15. What is the difference between primary sources and secondary research sources? Why is it important to look at a variety of different sources when you are gathering information? What can happen if you only use one source or one type of reference source in your research?

16. Amina is frustrated by her friends' and family's assumptions that she is romantically interested in Nico. She reflects, "But maybe I want to be friends with a boy without everyone assuming he's my boyfriend." Have you ever been in a situation like Amina? Do you think that it's harder for boys and girls to be friends as they get older? Explain your answers.

17. Describe the special bond that Amina has with her uncle Thaya Jaan. Do you have a family member whom you feel particularly close to? What interests or activities brought you together?

Guide prepared by Amy Jurskis, English Department Chair at Oxbridge Academy in Florida.

Turn the page for a sneak peek at

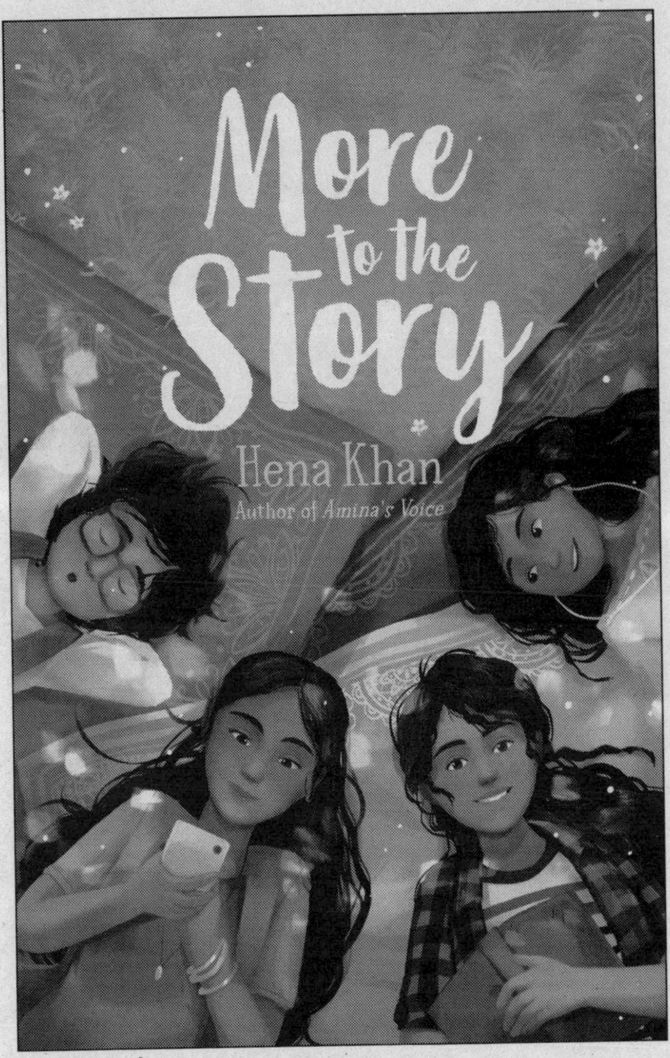

This is the worst Eid ever!" Aleeza flops onto the sofa and grabs the TV remote.

"You'll wrinkle your outfit," Bisma warns.

"I don't care," Aleeza says, then quickly adjusts her kameez beneath her. "It doesn't feel like Eid. Baba's not here. We were supposed to leave for the party like an hour ago. And now we're stuck at home, because people are coming over."

"Your whining doesn't make it any better," I snap at her. She's right that it's been a pretty disappointing day so far. Baba had to fly out for an interview in Maryland early this morning, before the rest of us went to the mosque for prayers. It's our first Eid without him, and everyone's been on edge. But it's only three o'clock in the afternoon. Maybe things will turn around.

"Come on, guys—it's Eid," Bisma pleads. "Can't you be nice to each other today?"

"*She* should be nice. Jam's always mean to me!" Aleeza shakes her finger at me, and her eyes fill up.

So much for things turning around. There's no way to sugarcoat it: My youngest sister is spoiled rotten. Aleeza's only ten, but that doesn't stop her from bossing around Bisma, who's a year older than her. And it doesn't matter to her that I'm thirteen and in middle school. Aleeza doesn't respect me like she should.

"Jameela!" Mama calls to me from the kitchen. "Can you go down and get the nice napkins? From the garage?"

"Okay." I'd rather face the lizards in the garage than listen to Aleeza whine for a second longer. Ever since Bisma saw a baby gecko scamper along the walls and freaked out like it had escaped from Jurassic Park, I'm the only one of us girls who dares to go in there alone.

The air inside the garage is suffocating, which isn't surprising, since it feels like five hundred degrees outside. This year Eid fell in August, the hottest month of the summer. Today also happens to be the kind of record-breaking scorcher of a day that earns Atlanta the nickname Hotlanta.

The jumbo pack of napkins is on a crowded shelf, next

to a box marked "JAMEELA'S STUFF: PRIVATE!!!" where I've stored my old journals and collection of last year's middle school newspapers. I was the only sixth grader who was an assistant editor and had an article in every issue of the paper, so I saved two copies of each. I resist the urge to carry the box inside so I can reread them, savoring each word like I want to.

Out of the corner of my eye I spot a lizard, frozen in place near the garage door opener. I decide it's going to be the subject of a future article in the *Mirza Memos*, the family newspaper I've been writing since I was nine years old. Maybe I'll research whether geckos have ever harmed humans, or how to get over the fear of creatures that resemble tiny alligators. If that includes hypnosis, I hope my sisters will let me try it out on them.

I make sure my box isn't at risk of getting crushed by the endless stream of things that flow out of our town house into the garage. Then I grab a stack of napkins and head upstairs to the kitchen. Mama is arranging mini samosas on a platter, while Maryam cuts the raspberry bars she made into neat squares.

"Can you put those on the table with this fruit?" Mama's brow furrows as she eyes the simple cotton shalwar kameez I threw on for Eid prayers earlier. "Aren't you going to change into your new clothes?"

This morning I hit my snooze button over and over, which left no time to iron the bright green outfit with sparkly gold thread work I'd left crumpled on my floor after trying it on last week. All I needed was a big star on my head, and I would have looked exactly like a walking Christmas tree decorated with tinsel. But since Mama's cousin in Pakistan had sent me the outfit, and because I knew it must have been expensive, I pretended to like it.

"Please say you will," Maryam adds. My older sister is elegant in her silvery-gray outfit with black embroidery. Her makeup, perfected after hours of watching tutorials on YouTube, is flawless. She's wearing a high bun, with wisps of loosened hairs that frame her cheekbones. As she bats her dark lashes at me, I squint at her, trying to tell if they're fake. She looks older than fifteen, and is glamorous.

"It's too hot for silk. Who's coming over, anyway?" I tuck a curl that escaped my ponytail behind my ear and try not to think about how my rolled-out-of-bed look compares to Maryam's. "Why do we need to impress them with fancy napkins?"

"Uncle Saeed. He's bringing his nephew. I'm just trying to make it special for Eid," Mama says.

I perk up when I hear "Uncle Saeed." He's Baba's

best friend, and our dentist. He's always armed with corny jokes and free toothbrushes.

When the doorbell rings, my mother gives me a gentle shove.

"Go change your clothes, and fix your hair, please," she urges. "There's a big stain on your kameez."

"It's fine," I say as I bound down the stairs for the door. "Uncle Saeed won't care. I'll change before the party."

I throw the door open.

"Eid Mubarak!" Uncle Saeed declares. He's holding a light blue box in his outstretched arms, and beads of sweat have already formed on his forehead. "Something sugary for the sweetest of days." Uncle often speaks as if he's quoting a Hallmark card.

"Eid Mubarak." I take the box and scan the label. Yes! It's from Sugar Kisses Bakery. Mama thinks it's overpriced and refuses to take us there. But when I tried their salted-caramel cupcake at Kayla's birthday party, it was literally one of the best desserts I've ever tasted. "Thank you! Come on in."

"Oof. It's too hot today. Eid Mubarak." Farah Auntie manages a weak smile, but her nose wrinkles slightly when she scans my hair and outfit.

"Are you feeling okay?" she whispers before hugging

me three times, enveloping me in the overpowering scent of her perfume. "Such simple clothes for Eid?"

"I'm great." I brush off Auntie's questions, since she's always one to gently point out how I dress too plainly for parties. Or weddings. Or Eid. If I were wearing my tinsel-tree getup, I'm sure I'd hear "Oh mashallah, *today* you look nice," no matter how uncomfortable or sweaty I felt. I've learned to let her and the other aunties comment about me, and then gush over Maryam. She puts enough effort into dressing up for both of us.

Uncle clears his throat.

"Jameela, this is my nephew, Ali, from London."

A tall boy with curly hair steps out from behind his uncle. I don't know anything about Pakistani fashion, but his crisp blue shalwar kameez with silver buttons isn't like the plain beige- or tan-colored ones Baba and Uncle wear. That, along with the way he's shielding his eyes from the bright light, makes it seem like he could be posing for the cover of my mom's glossy South Asian lifestyle magazine, *Libas*. I almost want to laugh.

"Asalaamualaikum," he says to me, extending his hand like a grown-up, although he can't be much older than me. "Pleasure to meet you." Ali's accent is definitely British, and his voice is deeper than I expected it to be.

“Wa . . . waalaikum asalaam,” I stammer as his dark eyes pierce mine. Suddenly I have another vision of how disheveled I must appear, and my cheeks heat up from more than the hot sun. I offer a limp handshake, try to cover up the stain on my shirt by folding it over, and gesture toward the stairs.

“Come on in. It’s a lot cooler inside. Everyone’s upstairs,” I mumble. “I have to . . . um. I’ll be right back. I just have to change and um, get ready.”

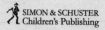